WORTHY OF LOVE

BOOK THREE OF THE DISCOVERING US SERIES

C.L. COLLIER

Cover Design by Amy Queau, Q Designs

Editing by Jenny Sims, Editing 4 Indies

❀ Created with Vellum

I dedicate this book to all my readers. I apologize it took so long for me to release this book.
I hope you enjoy it!

PROLOGUE

Brady

*T*his can't be fucking happening. It's like a nightmare I can't wake up from. Scott, my best friend since we were in the police academy together, is currently fighting for his life. He's the father of a baby girl, and he has another one on the way. We've been through a lot together over the years, and this can't be the end for him. He *has* to pull through.

But it's not just Scott in an operating room. Two more of our brothers are also in surgery at the moment, and a third one never made it to the hospital. Some fuckhead ambushed the officers responding to his wife's 911 call after he used her as his punching bag. The only saving grace in this whole situation is that the officers returned fire on the fucker, shooting him fatally.

Officers crowd the hospital waiting room. Reporters wait outside the building, anxiously awaiting an update. We're *all* waiting for an update from the doctors. It's impossible to relax and be patient because we want answers *now*.

I look across the room at Scott's ex-wife, Brooke, and his girlfriend, Lisa. Brooke and Scott's divorce was finalized recently,

1

and she's the mother of his daughter, Ellie. Lisa has only been his girlfriend for a few months now and is pregnant with his baby. It blows my mind that these two women are sitting together and comforting each other right now. Talk about forgiveness, under-standing, and being completely selfless. Amazing.

When a doctor makes his way into the room, everyone grows silent. He speaks quietly to the family of Marc Andrews. We can't hear what he's saying, but the relief that washes over Marc's wife's face says it all: he's going to be okay.

A short time later, another doctor appears and asks for Doug Lucas's family. I can tell his wife gets good news as well. Now we're just waiting to hear about Scott, and the suspense is killing me.

To pass the time, I pace around the room, occasionally stop-ping to chat with other officers. I also spend time talking with Brooke and Lisa. Brooke's boyfriend, Ryan, seems like a good guy for her. I don't agree with what Scott did to Brooke and how he let their marriage fall apart, so I'm glad to see her happy and moving on with her life.

When Scott's surgeon finally comes into the room and we get the news that he'll make a full recovery, tears spring to my eyes. I'm so happy and overwhelmed with emotion to know my friend will be okay. The entire room seems to breathe a collective sigh of relief.

As I drive home later, I'm overcome with emotion again. Only this time, it's for myself and what this job entails. I love being a police officer, but tonight has been a wake-up call for me. Police officers lose their lives every day, but it's becoming more and more common. My dad was a police officer—he was actually the chief of police in my hometown before he retired—and I grew up wanting to be just like him and his friends. Sure, I knew the risks that came with the job, but something has changed in the past few years, and those risks are far more realistic now. I'm only thirty-four years old. I don't have a wife or kids yet, but it's always been in my plans to have a family someday. Seeing what Marc, Doug, and Scott's families had to go through tonight has made me think twice. I don't want my future wife to be put through what they were. Or, worse, what David Jackson's family was told when the officers arrived at their home tonight to tell them he had been killed in the line of duty.

But I love the job. It's the only thing I've ever wanted to do. I don't even know what other career I could do because I've never pictured myself doing anything else. I love being a police officer and helping my community. Maybe I just need a change of scenery.

Maybe I need to get out of the big city.

Maybe I should move back home.

KELSEY

$\mathcal{T}$he cold swig of lemonade feels good going down my parched throat. I sink into my comfy, cushioned chair on my back patio and relax for the first time in months. I'm finally living back in my hometown. I've wanted to make this move for a couple of years now, but work has kept me in Seattle. High school counselor jobs are few and far between, so I've had to wait for one to open at Yelm High, my alma mater. When one finally popped up, I did everything I could to make sure the job was mine, and luck was on my side. I was so excited to move back to the small town I grew up in, so I didn't waste any time after they offered me the job. I found an apartment immediately, and as soon as my summer break started last week, I moved in.

For the past few years, I've worked as a high school counselor in Seattle. It's been okay, but after living in the Seattle area while attending college, I discovered I'm really not a big city girl. Yelm is fairly close to Washington's state capitol and city life, but it's still out of the hustle and bustle and where I prefer to be. I started feeling claustrophobic and anxious in the daily traffic jams I had to endure in Seattle, and being around *that* many people just made me crazy. Give me a town with just one main street and a few stoplights, and I'm good.

It's funny how things change. I wanted out of this town when I was a teenager. However, to say I made bad choices back then would be an understatement. Some memories will haunt me forever, but I felt even more lost and haunted in the city. I've learned to love myself and respect my family again, and I depend on their support more than I ever thought I would.

The irony that I'll be working as a counselor at the very school I was kicked out of isn't lost on me. I didn't graduate from Yelm High School, but now I'm going to be helping the students who go there and hope to make a difference in their lives. I went into this profession to give back to the community and help the teens who choose the wrong path in life, like I did. Luckily, I had some extraordinary counselors—in and out of the school system —who helped pull me out of my dark days as a teen. There's no telling how I would have ended up without all the counseling I went through.

One of the perks—probably the best one—of being a high school counselor is getting the summer off. Now that I've moved into my new apartment, I can relax and enjoy the rest of my break. I have to report back to school in August, and I'm looking forward to starting my new job and meeting all my colleagues. Some of the teachers I had when I was a student still work there, and I can't wait to show them how much I've worked to get my life back together. I'm truly grateful that the new administration decided to give me a chance and hire me. It helped that I had excellent references from my previous job.

Yelm has certainly changed a lot since I was a teenager. Like most small towns, it has seen a growth spurt over the past few years. More and more people like the idea of living away from the city and commuting to work. Though Yelm is still fairly small, a lot more businesses have moved in, and houses have popped up in recent years, adding to the population of the school district. When I was in school, we only had two counselors; I'm now one of four. In fact, the surge in the school's population led to the opening for the position of the fourth counselor at Yelm High.

I sit in my chair, basking in the sun on this unusually hot June day. We usually have to wait until mid-July to enjoy *real* summer weather here in the Pacific Northwest, but today is a beautiful exception. I close my eyes and soak up the sunshine. I was happy to find this apartment in a new complex in town. My unit is on the ground level with a small patio out back. For days like today, it's perfect to sit outside on and relax. My phone buzzes on the table next to me, so I pick it up to check my text. It's my brother, Nolan.

Nolan: 4th of July BBQ, our house, 6:00. Hope you can make it!

I text him back to tell him I'll be there. I already knew he was having this party, and he should know I'm planning to go. My brother, the family man with the perfect wife and daughter, hosts a Fourth of July party every year, and I haven't missed one yet. I always enjoy spending time with my family, especially my brother's three-year-old daughter, Emmy. She is the cutest little thing, and I love being her auntie. I can spoil her to death, play with her and have fun, then hand her back to her parents and go on with my life. I'm just not the marrying, child-bearing type. Being a high school counselor and auntie are enough for me. My parents wish I would settle down with a nice man and have babies of my own. No, thank you.

I come from a very loving family. Mom is a high school math teacher, and Dad is a civil engineer. Nolan followed in Dad's footsteps. His wife, Teresa, is a stay-at-home mom with Emmy now, although she, too, used to be a civil engineer. That was how she and Nolan met; they used to work together. Mom still teaches at the high school I actually graduated from, which is in another nearby small town. She's taught at Tenino High for almost thirty years.

My phone buzzes again, and I see another text from my brother.

Nolan: Great! Can't wait to see you. Emmy is looking forward to seeing her auntie Kelsey.

Attached to the text is a picture of Emmy with a big smile on her face. She is quite the little character and melts my heart.

Finishing my lemonade, I head back into my apartment to make dinner. Cooking is a hobby of mine. I discovered I had a knack for it when I moved out to go to college and actually had to fend for myself. Nolan appreciated it, too, since I moved in with him at the time. It saved him from his dinner rotations of frozen meals, ramen noodles, and mac and cheese. Tonight, I'm making tuna avocado boats, a healthy recipe I found online that I love.

Later, after I finish dinner and while I'm cleaning up my kitchen, I get another text from my brother.

Nolan: Hey, do you remember Brady Danner?

I roll my eyes and start to type out a response. Of course, I remember his best friend growing up. His best friend, whose father was the Tenino chief of police. In fact, if I remember correctly, I think Nolan said Brady became a cop in Portland or someplace down in Oregon. I guess the apple doesn't fall far from the tree.

Me: Yes. Why do you ask?

Nolan: He just moved back to Yelm. He's renting an apartment at the same complex as you.

Well, that's a coincidence. Maybe I'll see him around here, though I probably wouldn't recognize him if I did. It's been over a decade since I saw him last. He was friends with Nolan, but after they graduated high school, Brady moved away for college. I don't recall him ever coming back to visit Nolan after that.

Me: That's nice. Would I even recognize him? I can't remember the last time I saw him.

Nolan: He's coming to the bbq on the 4th, so you'll see him then.

My mind wanders back, trying to remember what I knew about Brady, besides what his dad did for a living. He played sports with Nolan and was always hanging around our house. I never paid that much attention to my brother's friends, though. They were older than me, and my philosophy at the time was that they weren't very interesting if they were friends with my brother.

Nolan is two years older than I am. Even through my difficult times, we've always gotten along well. He was always there to help, even when I was a complete disgrace. I may not be where I am today without Nolan; actually, my parents helped me throughout my life, too. I couldn't be more thankful for the family I have.

My phone vibrates again.

Nolan: He's single. ;-)

I roll my eyes. Of course Nolan has other motives. Like my parents, he'd like to see me settle down. I decide to ignore his text and don't reply. I can only tell my family so many times that I'm not interested in dating.

JULY 4TH

*a*t quarter after six, I pull up to Nolan's house. Several cars are already parked in his cul-de-sac, so the party must be off to a good start. I make my way to the front door with the little gift I brought for Emmy. The door swings open before I can even knock, and Emmy bolts out, throwing her arms around me.

"Auntie Kelsey!" she exclaims.

I bend to hug her in return. "Hey, squirt! How are you?"

She pulls back from me and looks at me with the sweetest smile on her face. "Good! I've been watching for you out the window!"

Teresa appears in the doorway and leans against the door-jamb. "Emmy has been *dying* for you to get here," she says with a chuckle.

I hold the small gift bag out for Emmy to take. "Well, I found this and thought you might like it."

Emmy's eyes get big as she looks at the gift bag. "For me?" she asks, moving her little hand to her chest as if she's shocked by my gesture.

I can't help but laugh at how adorable she is. "Yes, silly. Go ahead and take it!"

Emmy takes the gift bag from me and opens it. "Oh, my gosh!" Her little voice is full of excitement. I love my niece, and I love spoiling her. She is like my mini me.

Although I pray she's smarter than I was when she becomes a teenager.

Emmy pulls the pink sequin coin purse from the bag.

"Open it," I tell her.

She unzips the little purse, and her eyes light up once more. "Lipstick!" she squeals.

"Lip-gloss," I correct her. "Let's go inside, and I'll show you how to apply it."

I stand and follow Emmy into the house. I give Teresa a hug as I walk through the door.

"Thanks a lot," Teresa says sarcastically. "You spoil her too much."

"That's my job," I reply with a conspiratorial grin.

Teresa shakes her head and laughs. I love my sister-in-law. She's perfect for my brother, and she's an amazing mom to Emmy.

I follow Emmy into the family room, which is full of party guests. The French doors leading to the back patio are wide open, and I see several people outside as well. Emmy runs outside, and I see her find Grandma—my mom—and proudly show her the gift I brought her.

"Are you all settled into your apartment?" Teresa asks.

I turn to her and see she's handing me a Coke. She knows me so well.

"I am! I love it so far. It's nice being in a brand-new building. Everything is so shiny and new."

"It's so good to have you back in Yelm," she says with a kind smile. "Nolan and I are really glad you got the job and moved back."

"Me, too." I take a drink of the Coke, then follow Teresa

outside to the patio.

"Kelsey!" Dad exclaims, then walks toward me with his arms out. I hug my dad. He's always shown me unconditional love, even when I was unlovable.

After saying hello to my brother and a few other friends, I settle into a patio chair next to my mom. "Are you settled into your apartment now?" she asks.

"Pretty much. I have everything unpacked, and it's starting to feel more like home now."

"Good," Mom replies. "I'm so happy to have you back here in Yelm."

"It's great to be back," I say with a smile.

We continue talking about our summer plans before Emmy interrupts us, climbing onto my lap. "Auntie Kelsey, I want to see fireworks!"

Mom and I chuckle. "Well, we have to wait for it to get dark first. Otherwise, we won't really be able see the fireworks."

"That's what my dad said," she says, sounding defeated. Then she climbs off my lap, and without another word, she runs off onto the grass to play with some other kids who are here.

Nolan appears and pulls up a chair next to me. "Hey, there," he says to Mom and me.

"Hello again," I reply. Although I said hi to him before, we haven't had a chance to sit down and talk.

"Burgers and dogs are ready to eat. Everything is set out in the kitchen. Feel free to help yourselves," he informs us, then takes a drink of his beer.

"Thanks for letting us know," Mom says. "I think I'll go get a plate."

"I'll get some in a bit," I say, not really feeling hungry yet. Mom retreats into the house.

"I'm glad you came over," Nolan says to me.

"I wouldn't miss it," I reply. "I never do. I enjoy this party every year."

Nolan glances at his phone, then continues. "Brady Danner is going to be here soon."

I roll my eyes at my brother. "Okay ..." After Nolan mentioned Brady in his text, I knew he was going to try to set us up. I don't like being set up because I don't like dating, period. I've tried over the years, but it always brings back too many painful memories. I've tried to get help in counseling, but I gave up. I've made peace with the fact that I'm just not meant to be in a relationship.

"I'm not trying to set you up," Nolan adds. "I just thought since you both recently moved back to town, you live in the same apartment complex, and you're both single ... it couldn't hurt to introduce you. At the very least, maybe you'll make a new friend who also happens to be your neighbor."

I cock an eyebrow at my brother, letting him know I'm not stupid. I see right through his plan. *Sure, he's not trying to set me up.*

"Hey," he says, shrugging his shoulders as if to apologize, "it's good to have a friendly neighbor. What if you need to borrow a cup of sugar?"

I roll my eyes again and chuckle. "Sure, Nolan." Shaking my head, I know I can't escape my introduction to Brady tonight. "I don't mind meeting him, of course. But please understand I'm just not in a good place to date right now."

Nolan sighs, clearly exasperated. "When will you be in a good place to date, Kelsey? You've been using that excuse for years now."

I look away from my brother. I can't tell him, or anyone in my family, the true reason I can't date. They would never look at me the same again. "I'm just getting settled here. Just don't pressure me, okay?"

"Okay," he says, patting my knee and drawing my attention back to him. Nolan gives a small smile, and I can tell my brother just wants the best for me. I wish my life was different.

Just then, Mom returns with a plate of food. "Kelsey, go help yourself before all the good stuff is gone! There's quite a spread in there."

I smile at her and use this as an excuse to escape my conversation with Nolan. "It looks good. I'll go check it out."

Suddenly feeling hungry at the sight of all the food in the kitchen, I fill my plate and chat with some of Nolan and Teresa's friends; people I've met here over the years on the Fourth of July. Their friends are all so kind, congratulating me on my new job and commenting on how wonderful it is that I'm living in Yelm again. Just as I'm about to walk back outside, I spot someone new walk in the room, and Teresa is quick to greet him.

"Brady!" I hear her say to the man setting a six-pack of beer on the kitchen counter.

Damn, *that's* Brady Danner? He's sure a lot more handsome than he was in high school!

Avert your eyes, Kelsey! I quickly turn and continue where I was going before being momentarily distracted. I walk outside and sit with Mom and Nolan again, who are now discussing how Dad is considering retiring by the end of the year. He's been contemplating this for a couple of years now, but he just continues to work. He really loves his job, but he's now one of the oldest employees at his firm, and most of his good buddies have retired.

Just as I'm about to join the conversation, Teresa's voice booms from the doorway. "Nolan! Brady's here!"

Nolan turns and smiles at his wife. "Great!" he replies to her, then turns to Mom and me. "Excuse me, ladies," he says as he stands to go greet his friend. I don't miss the pointed look he gives me before he disappears into the house.

Mom starts then. "Nolan was telling me that Brady lives in the same apartment complex as you. That's a coincidence!"

I finish chewing the potato salad in my mouth before replying. "It's either a coincidence, or just the simple fact that Yelm doesn't have a whole lot of places to rent." I chuckle to let my mom know I'm joking.

"I suppose so," she says. "Though Yelm is growing more and more by the day."

We continue eating for a few minutes before Nolan appears again, this time with Brady by his side. "Mom, Kelsey, do you remember Brady Danner?" he asks.

I wipe my mouth with my napkin and realize Brady is even more attractive up close. The Mariners baseball cap on his head isn't helping matters, either. I've always found that a baseball cap adds about ten points of hotness to a man. But I can tell that Brady is handsome even without the hat. His friendly smile and kind blue eyes do it for me.

Jesus, Kelsey! Get a grip!

"Of course," Mom replies. "It's so good to see you again, Brady!"

Brady puts out his hand to shake Mom's. "It's good to see you again, too, Mrs. Richards."

"Oh please, just call me Mary," Mom replies with a smile.

Then Brady turns toward me. "Hey, Kelsey. Good to see you again."

I smile and hope the lust I'm feeling toward Brady isn't written all over my face. "It's good to see you, too." Thank God he doesn't shake my hand like he did Mom's. I'm not sure what touching this fine man would do to me at the moment. I may not want to date anyone, but I'm not blind, and I *am* a healthy, heterosexual female. *Fuck—his body is fit, too.*

"Have a seat," Nolan says, offering Brady the chair he was sitting in before; the one right next to me.

"Okay," Brady replies before planting himself in the chair, which now seems much closer than it did when Nolan was sitting there.

Nolan pulls up another chair to join us. "Brady, you and Kelsey live in the same apartments."

"That's what you told me," Brady replies and looks at me.

I raise my eyebrows, looking at Brady. "What a coincidence."
Or not ...

Brady's smile just about does me in. His dimples are just too much. Why don't I remember this about him when we were younger? I never thought of him as good looking, but then again, I didn't really pay attention to my brother and his friends.

Brady brings a bottle of beer to his lips and takes a drink. I have to turn away to keep from ogling.

"Nolan said you're working for the Tenino Police Department now," Mom says to him.

"That's right," Brady replies, setting the bottle on his knee.

I'm trying really hard not to stare at him.

"Maybe I'll see you around town once school starts. I'm still teaching at the high school there, you know," Mom adds.

"Oh, that's right. I'm sure I'll see you at some point. It's a small town." Brady smiles at Mom. God, he's so friendly.

"It's so great that you're working for the same department your dad worked for," Mom says. "What made you decide to come back, anyway?"

I look at Brady's face again and notice a slight look of *something* cross his features at Mom's question. I don't know what it is, but maybe a hint of sorrow? It was so quick that most people probably wouldn't have noticed it, but I've always been intuitive to other people's emotions.

"I was tired of working in the big city and wanted a change of pace," Brady tells Mom. To me, it sounds like a canned response; something he's had to repeat time and time again. Almost rehearsed. *Interesting.* "Portland was great, but I missed being home. I always wanted to follow in Dad's footsteps, so this is really the perfect transition for me."

"Well, everyone's glad you moved back," Nolan says.

"Thanks, man," Brady replies before taking another drink of his beer.

I look at Mom, and she actually smirks at me. *Great.* I know what she's thinking. She's now on the same team as Nolan and wants to set me up. I give her a look, trying to tell her to *stop*, then go back to eating the potato salad on my plate.

"How do you like your new apartment? I wonder if it's close to Kelsey's?" Mom asks.

I jerk my eyes up to meet Mom's again, but she's looking at Brady, not me. I continue to chew my food, somewhat grateful my mouth is full at the moment so I don't say something I would regret later.

"I really like it," Brady replies. I look over at him and smile— the best I can with food in my mouth, anyway. He's looking at me as well, and I hope to God I don't look as awkward as I feel. "What unit are you in?" he asks me.

I swallow the potato salad—which is delicious, by the way; I idly wonder if I can find out who made it and get the recipe— then answer, "J-17. What about you?"

"S-10," he replies. "I guess we're a few buildings away from each other."

"I can't believe how big your apartment complex is," Mom pipes in. "I never thought Yelm would see such a boom in its population."

I nod in agreement because it's true. The apartment complex has twenty buildings with either six or eight apartments in each, depending on their size. It's the largest complex our town has ever seen, and most of the apartments have been rented out already.

"So, Kelsey, I hear you're the new counselor at Yelm High," Brady says. When I turn my attention to him once again, I realize that I liked the way my name rolled off his tongue. I've never considered someone's voice sexy before, but that's the perfect way to describe Brady's. *God, what is wrong with me?*

"Yes, I am," I reply, trying not to give anymore thought to his voice. "I can't wait to start!"

"That's great," he says. "It must be weird to go back to the same school you graduated from."

I chuckle, unintentionally. Brady must not remember that I was kicked out of Yelm. After all, he and Nolan were already in college when that happened, and Brady had gone out of state. Honestly, I don't even know if he and Nolan were still in contact at that time.

Before I can tell him myself, Mom speaks up. "Actually, Kelsey graduated from Tenino. She transferred there her senior year and went to school with me every day."

I inwardly cringe at Mom's words. Even after all these years, I can't help but feel a twinge of shame at the fact that I was kicked out of a school for drugs, and my mom had to beg her principal to allow me to finish my senior year at Tenino. I know I'm way past that now, but I can't help feeling that way, especially in front of my family.

"Is that right?" Brady says, surprised. "I had no idea."

Taking a deep breath, I decide to be straightforward with my answer. After all, there's no need to hide anything after all these years, considering I'm not the messed-up teenager I once was. Brady must know that his dad arrested me ... at least, I think he knows.

"Yes. Actually, I *had* to transfer to Tenino. I really didn't have a choice, considering Yelm expelled me."

Brady's eyes practically bulge out of his head. I wish I could record the shocked look on his face! Maybe he *doesn't* know about my criminal years ...

"You got expelled?" he asks, seeming to be completely unaware of my past. Well, this'll be interesting filling him in.

"You didn't know that?" I ask, looking back and forth between Nolan and Brady. Nolan's face says *oh shit* all over it. I can tell he never told his friend about his sister's wild ways.

Rubbing the back of his neck as an obvious nervous gesture, Nolan says, "I guess Brady and I lost touch for a while in college, and I never told him."

I try not to smirk as I laugh to myself in my head. Suddenly feeling snarky, I wonder how both Brady and Nolan will react to what I'm about to say. I look directly at Brady, and ask, "Didn't your dad ever tell you he arrested me?"

Brady's jaw nearly hits the floor, and he almost drops his beer, catching his grip before letting it fall. I can't help but snicker, and then Mom speaks up.

"It wasn't her finest moment," she explains. I'm sure she still feels the need to explain how her daughter became such a disappointment. I look at her, and she gives me a sad smile, as if to say, *"I still love you."*

I smile in return, knowing we're past that time in our lives— thank goodness—and open my mouth to respond, but Brady beats me to it.

"First of all, you were arrested? Second of all, my *dad* arrested you?"

I nod my head, then reply, "Yes. Actually, I was arrested more than once. The first time was by the Yelm police for underage drinking. The second time was your dad."

This time, Brady's beer actually slips from his fingers and falls to the ground. "Shit," he mumbles as he scrambles to pick it up.

I chuckle, but again, Mom has to add an explanation. "Kelsey went through a rough time and was hanging around the wrong crowd. We were lucky things didn't turn out worse for her, and that she's still here all this time later to talk about it." She reaches her hand toward me and grips my knee, giving me a warm smile. "She turned her life around, and we couldn't be more proud of her," she adds, looking me straight in the eye as she says it.

It actually chokes me up. My joking behavior is sobered, and I take Mom's hand in mine. "Thank you, Mom."

"I had no idea," Brady says. Mom takes her hand from mine, and I turn my attention back toward him.

"Yeah, the summer before my junior year of high school, my best friend moved away. I was sad, and I felt as if I didn't have anyone to hang out with. Then, one day I was at the park and met a girl my age who had just moved to town. We became fast friends, but I quickly discovered she was trouble. It didn't deter me, though; instead, I was intrigued and just wanted to have a friend. So I started getting into a little trouble with her ... which led to more trouble ... which eventually led to a heroin addiction. That's the very short, edited version, anyway."

Brady's eyes widen a fraction more. "Wow, Kelsey. I'm glad you got your life back on track. I never knew you went through all this, and my dad never told me about your arrests."

Suddenly, Teresa appears to my side, interrupting our conversation. "Hey, guys," she says, completely unaware of our heavy conversation. Honestly, I'm a little relieved to have a way out of it now. As much as I was enjoying shocking Brady with my history, it's never an easy story to tell. "Nolan, did you tell Brady about the get-together at Rick's Saturday night?"

In my opinion, Ricks, the bar in town frequented by people our age, is the only acceptable one in town. Our town has several to choose from, including the dive bar where the old-timers hang out, the biker bar, the country western bar, and the heavy metal bar. Yelm has something for everyone.

"I was going to tell him, but I haven't had a chance to yet," Nolan explains, then he goes on to tell Brady about the get-together Saturday night, where a bunch of people are going to hear a band called Riser play. I guess the bass player went to school with Brady and Nolan, so their former classmates are going to support him.

"You're welcome to come, too, Kelsey," Teresa adds, patting my shoulder. I look up at her, standing next to my chair. She smiles at me, then flicks a subtle, quick glance toward Brady. I get what she's hinting at, and I roll my eyes at her.

Great, now Mom, Nolan, and *Teresa are going to try to set me up!*

"Yeah, you should come," Nolan says to me.

I look at my brother, and reply, "I'll see if I can make it."

KELSEY

*S*aturday night rolls around, and I find myself getting ready to go to Rick's. I don't usually hit the bar scene, and when I do, I still don't drink. I gave that up at the ripe young age of seventeen, and I'm perfectly content in life without it.

I drive myself the short distance to Rick's on Yelm's main drag. Luckily, I find a parking space in the lot right behind the bar, so I don't have to parallel park on the street. I'm not the best at parallel parking, and I prefer to avoid it whenever I can.

As I walk toward the entrance of Rick's, I can hear a band playing inside as well as some people whooping and hollering. It sounds like a fun time, and I'm actually looking forward to this night out with my brother, Teresa, and their friends.

Oh, and Brady. I can at least enjoy being in his presence and admire his good looks for a couple of hours.

As I walk in, Teresa immediately sees me and waves me over to their table. Actually, they have two tables shoved together with about ten people sitting around them. The whole place is packed, with all other tables taken and people dancing near the stage where the band is playing.

"Hi, Kelsey," Teresa says, standing as I approach. She wraps me in a hug, then turns to the others at the table and introduces me. "If you don't know her already, this is Nolan's sister, Kelsey."

Everyone says hi, giving a friendly wave or nod. Teresa pulls up a chair next to her for me to sit on. Nolan is at the other end of the table, talking with friends, but I don't notice Brady here. I wonder if he's coming tonight?

The next hour goes by, and it dawns on me that this is the best night out I've had in ages. The band is incredibly good, and the crowd's energy is contagious. All of Nolan and Teresa's friends are fun to hang out with as I usually find their friends to be. This is exactly what I needed tonight instead of curling up on my couch and binge-watching Netflix at home ... *again.*

Just as the band starts to play one of my favorite songs from the 90s, I feel a hand on my left shoulder. I turn my head at the same time Teresa looks back, and I'm surprised to find the hand belongs to Brady. I'm even more surprised to find how attracted I am to him tonight. Unlike at the Fourth of July party, he's not wearing a hat, and his brown hair is just messy enough to look sexy. His blue eyes even seem to smile at me.

"Hey, Brady!" Teresa says, and I notice he had placed his other hand on her shoulder when he walked up behind us to get our attention. She stands to give him a hug, then Nolan notices he's here.

"Hey, man!" Nolan calls from the other end of the table before standing and walking over to greet him. I turn my attention back to the band and take a sip of my Pepsi.

Looking at Teresa as she sits again, I notice Brady takes a seat next to Nolan at the other end of the table. Brady happens to look in my direction, and our eyes meet. He smiles ... a sexy sort of smile. My stomach flip flops, and it takes me by surprise. I turn my eyes back to the band, and I immediately regret it. Was I just rude to Brady by not smiling back? Maybe he didn't notice. But I don't look at him again.

Not yet.

Not for at least a couple of minutes, anyway.

I literally can't help but feel a pull toward Brady, and it's nothing like I've ever felt before. I can't stop myself from looking in his direction again, and while he's in the middle of a conversation with Nolan, he immediately looks at me, as well. When our eyes meet, his lips curve into a smile, and I smile in return. Then he looks back at Nolan, who's still in the middle of telling him something.

"He's a good-looking guy." Teresa's voice snaps me out of my reverie.

"What? Who?" I ask, trying to act as nonchalant as I can. I hope she didn't catch me admiring Brady, not to mention our subtle exchange.

Teresa's elbow bumps mine, and she scoffs. "Don't try to act like nothing just happened between you and Brady."

Okay. She noticed.

I shake my head, hoping to write it off as an innocent friendly gesture.

Teresa rolls her eyes and leans in closer to me so only I can hear what she's about to say. "You cannot seriously tell me as a straight, warm-blooded female that Brady Danner is not an attractive man."

I can't help the giggle that escapes my mouth. As much as I want to deny it, she's right; he is extremely attractive.

Teresa giggles, too. "Okay, then," she says. "Now the question is, how do we get you two together?"

I look at my sister-in-law as if she's crazy. She can't possibly be serious. "What do you mean?"

"Come on, Kelsey. He's single … you're single. You're both new to town again, and you happen to live just a few buildings apart from each other. If you ask me, this has *setup* written all over it!"

I let out a hearty laugh, which draws the attention of everyone at the table, including Brady. When I catch his eye, I calm myself, but he smiles wider than I've ever seen before. My hand flies to my throat as I try to wipe the smile from my own face, embarrassed at the attention I've drawn.

"Take it easy down there!" Nolan shouts at me in a joking manner.

Teresa nudges me with her elbow again, then leans in and whispers in my ear, "This is going to happen."

Before I can stop her, Teresa stands and walks over to my brother, leaning down to whisper in his ear. Thank God, Brady has turned his attention to the band on stage. I can only imagine what Teresa is saying to Nolan right now. Is she really cooking up a plan to set me up with Brady? My heart races, and I'm full of nerves now. Maybe I should just go home and avoid all this?

I watch as Nolan nods his head in agreement with whatever his wife is whispering in his ear. Then he looks at me and smirks. Shit! What are they planning? My palms now feel clammy. I can't remember the last time I had these feelings. Honestly, probably not since I was a teenager.

I try to pry my eyes away, but I can't. I watch as Nolan gets up and seems to ask the guys sitting closest to him if they want another round of drinks. Brady nods his head, as do a couple of other guys. Nolan nudges Brady's shoulder and says something to him, then Brady gets up and walks to the bar with him. *What's going on?*

Teresa takes Brady's seat after they walk away, then playfully waves to me, winking as she does. I discreetly flip her off in return, and she laughs, shaking her head at me. I take a deep breath and turn my head so I can see what my brother is up to now. Luckily, from where I'm sitting, I have a view without it being obvious that I'm looking at the bar. Also, Nolan's and Brady's back are to me, so they can't see me watching them anyway.

I see them ordering drinks, and the bartender brings four bottles of beer to them. Nolan and Brady take one in each hand, but then Nolan says something to Brady, nodding his head in the direction of our table. Who knows what he said, but then they both walk back and deliver the beers to the guys who asked for one. However, with Teresa now in his seat, Brady doesn't have anywhere to sit. That doesn't deter him, though. He looks up at me and heads in my direction.

Oh.

"Hey, do you need another drink?" he asks when he reaches my side.

I glance at my half-full glass of Pepsi. "No, I'm good," I reply, looking back up at Brady, wondering if he's going to sit in Teresa's vacant seat next to me. My heart is racing. *I'm nervous.*

"Okay," Brady says as he sits next to me. Getting a whiff of his cologne, which smells of spice and wood, all my senses are in overdrive. It's almost as if static electricity zaps between us, and I wonder if he feels it, too.

"Are you having fun?" Brady asks, taking a drink of his beer but keeping his eyes on me as he does.

My mouth suddenly goes dry, looking at this fine man next to me. I've never had this kind of reaction to a man before, and it's starting to freak me out.

"Yeah," I stammer, finding my voice. "Are you?"

"Yeah, the band is pretty good," he says, nodding toward the stage. They're playing another popular song from the 90s, but I can't remember the name of it. Brady's eyes settle on his beer bottle in front of him, and he rubs his thumb against the label. After a moment, he looks back at me and continues. "I can't remember the last time I went out with friends like this."

His comment surprises me for some reason. "Is that right?"

"Yeah, I tend to work a lot, and when I do have a night off, I usually stay at home and relax."

I nod my head, realizing that his job must be beyond stressful. I can't imagine what it must be like to deal with criminals all the time.

"However, I plan on spending more time with friends now that I'm back in Yelm. Living here is a lot different than Portland."

Remembering his seemingly canned response about moving back when we were at Nolan's party, I decide to ask him about it. "What was it like working in Portland?"

Again, like at Nolan's, I notice Brady slightly react to my question, but he doesn't miss a beat in answering me. "It was busy, and there was always something. I was never bored, that's for sure," he says with a chuckle.

"It must be really stressful being a cop."

Brady looks down as he nods. "You could say that."

"You must see a lot of crazy things."

He chuckles again, then looks back at me. "You have no idea. What about you, though? Being a school counselor must be pretty stressful as well."

I chuckle, thinking of all the kids who have stressed me out over the years. As much as I love my job, it's definitely more stressful than I'd like. "You could say that. I guess we both have stressful jobs."

We spend the next hour talking with each other, telling silly stories about our jobs and not the stressful ones. We laugh together, and I discover I'm having more fun than I've had in a long time. Not only that, but Brady's laughter is infectious, and he looks even more sexy when he does it. I couldn't be more turned on if I tried, but this is new territory for me. As much as I'm enjoying myself, I have no idea where this is going, and that terrifies me.

When I see Nolan and Teresa stand as if they're about to leave, I start to panic. I've wondered how tonight would end, and now it's time to find out. Will Brady want to leave now, too? Or will he stay?

They make their way over to us, and Brady and I look up at

them. "We're going home now. It was good to see you, man," Nolan says, patting Brady on the back.

"Thanks for inviting me," Brady replies.

Nolan looks at me. "I'm glad you came out, sis. Don't stay out too late." He smirks, then bends over to give me a hug.

"You don't need to worry about me," I reply as I embrace my brother.

"No, not anymore," he says, giving me a squeeze. His words actually choke me up, so I swallow to keep my emotions at bay.

Nolan stands again, taking his wife's hand. "See you guys later," Teresa says as she waves to Brady and me. Then they turn and leave.

Brady and I look at each other, and I wonder if he's as nervous as I am. What's next? I don't know what to expect, and honestly, I don't really know what *I* want. I'm enjoying my time with him, but maybe we should just be friends?

Oh God. What if that's all Brady wants, and I've been misreading him all night? I am *not* used to this sort of thing!

Before I can stew over this any longer, Brady speaks up. "I'm having a really good time."

Something about the way Brady says that, and the way he looks at me—almost as if he's a nervous teenager talking to his crush—makes it impossible not to smile. "I am, too," I reply, feeling my cheeks blush.

Actually, maybe *I* look like a teenager talking to her crush, too.

Brady smiles, but then we're interrupted by another couple at our table who has decided to leave. Before we know it, we're the only ones left sitting here.

"It's getting late," Brady says, glancing at the thick watch on his wrist. Jesus, even his wrist is sexy.

Without really thinking, I automatically reply, "Yeah, I should probably get going."

"Me, too," Brady says. "I had a lot of fun tonight, Kelsey." He reaches his hand out and touches mine on the table.

His touch takes me by surprise, and I can't help but swoon. I've never had a reaction like this before, and my heart is racing in my chest. I don't know what to say or do, so I'm relieved when Brady squeezes my hand, then lets go.

"Let me walk you to your car," he says kindly. We both stand and gather our things.

Brady and I walk outside, not saying a word. It's an awkward silence, but I don't know what to say. I wonder if he's tongue-tied as well, and that's why he's not talking? My heart is still beating out of my chest, and I feel my palms getting sweaty. I truly am like a teenager because I have such limited experience in the dating world.

When we reach my car, Brady says, "Well, maybe I'll see you around. I hope to, anyway." He smiles at me, but I can tell he's nervous when he rubs the back of his neck. The realization that I'm not the only one feeling this way actually calms me.

"I'm sure we'll run into each other at some point, living in the same apartment complex and all," I reply.

Brady's smile widens, and butterflies pick up in my stomach. "Okay, well, I'll see you around then." Brady moves closer to me, and my breath hitches. To say I'm disappointed when he only gives me a hug and not a kiss would be an understatement. But his muscular arms around me feel oh, so good. As my hands touch his back, I can tell Brady is very fit. I can only imagine how sexy his body must look underneath his clothes.

As Brady pulls back, he says, "Good night, Kelsey." Then he walks toward his car.

"Good night," I stammer, watching him walk away. Then I turn and get in my car.

KELSEY

It's been three months since that night at Rick's, and Brady and I have bumped into each other a handful of times around the apartment complex and in town. Nothing has happened between us, but every time I see him, I can't help but feel a pull toward him. I just don't know what to do about it. If he was really interested in me, he'd make a move ... wouldn't he? I feel like a foreign exchange student, confused by our country's culture and traditions. I'm just as confused by the male species and how to date them.

School has started, and I love my new job! The staff I work with is great, and the students are amazing. Even the most troubled students I work with amaze me with their life stories and what they've endured. Abuse, neglect, homelessness, even rape ... yet they still come to school and don't give up. One girl, in particular, reminds me so much of myself in high school, and I hope I can help her stay off drugs and stay in school. Her name is Bridget, and she's an extremely bright girl who is just making bad choices. Although I don't usually have favorite students, she's kind of my favorite this year. The similarities between us are uncanny, and I just want to see her succeed.

It's Friday afternoon, and school just got out. I have some paperwork to do, but I should be able to leave in an hour or so. That's good timing for me; usually, I end up staying after school for at least a couple of hours to get caught up on things.

Just as I'm finishing, I get a text from Nolan.

Nolan: Meet us at Rick's tonight. Riser is playing again, and a bunch of people will be there!

I smile, remembering the last time I went to Rick's with Nolan, Teresa, and their friends to hear Riser play. I had a lot of fun ... especially talking with Brady. I haven't had a night out like that since, and I think it's just what I need.

I reply to Nolan.

Me: What time should I be there?

After getting all the details from Nolan, I clean up my desk, then head home. I wonder if Brady will be there tonight. I didn't ask my brother because I knew that would spark a million questions about my interest in his friend. Nolan hasn't tried to set me up again at all, so I don't want to give him any ideas. However, maybe I wouldn't mind if he tried to get Brady and me together again ... maybe.

I make a quick dinner, then decide to take a bubble bath before getting ready for my night out. As I'm soaking in the warm bubbles, I think about what I would do if Brady actually showed interest in me. I can't remember the last time I even kissed a man. Will I remember how, or will it turn into an embarrassing disaster? A sense of panic wells up in me, and I take a deep breath to ease my nerves. It doesn't make the butterflies in my stomach go away, though. *Shit!* Why do I have to be like this? Why can't I just be a normal woman who knows what the hell she's supposed to do when she's interested in a man?

Because of the past.

Damn. I take another deep breath and sit up, hugging my knees. I wish I had known as a teenager just how much I was fucking my life up. Little did I realize how my stupid choices back then would continue to affect me over a decade later. I may be attracted to Brady Danner, but the reality is that he's too good for me. He's a police officer who upholds the law, and I'm just one of the people his own father arrested. Why would he ever be interested in me?

As I get out of the tub and begin to dry off, I conclude that Brady and I will *never* happen. The thought depresses me more than I expect it to, considering I never feel this way about men! Why do I feel this way about him? I don't even know if he's interested in me, or if he just sees me as a friend. It's been months since we last hung out. Why should I feel this sad about something that never even started?

I contemplate whether I should still go out tonight because I don't really feel in the mood anymore. In fact, I feel like a fool, thinking that I could possibly have a shot at flirting and having fun with Brady again tonight. If he was really interested in me, he would've contacted me by now, but he hasn't.

Just as I'm about to text Nolan and tell him I'm not coming, I get a text from him instead.

Nolan: *Brady will be there tonight. ;-)*

Oh, shit.

I shake my head and rub the back of my neck. Why does my

brother feel the need to tell me this? It's almost as if he was reading my mind and knew he had to tell me that to get me to go out. But what difference does it really make? Brady is not interested in me.

Me: *Okay...*
    Nolan: *Just thought you'd like to know. He's still single.*

Rolling my eyes, I hesitate before replying because I'm not quite sure what to say. I start to type out that I'm going to stay home after all, but Nolan replies before I can finish.

Nolan: *He asked if you were going to be there tonight.*

My fingers freeze, and my heart begins to pound as I re-read Nolan's text. Brady asked about me? *Why?* Why would he be interested in me? He hasn't said or done anything in the past three months to show he's interested. We only live a few buildings away from each other, and he's never pursued me.

But neither have I. Even though I've practically lusted after him ever since Nolan's Fourth of July party, I haven't exactly projected my interest in him, either.

That thought makes me stop in my tracks. Maybe it's not just up to Brady; maybe *I* could've done something these past few months to show him I want more than just a friendship. We're not in the Stone Age anymore. Men don't have to make the first move ... do they?

Frustrated with my lack of understanding of how to date, I let out an audible groan. Pulling my inner thoughts together and pushing my self-doubt aside, I decide to take a chance. After all, what's the worst that can happen?

Rejection.

Embarrassment.

Or the possibility of happiness. Who the hell knows? I've never put myself out there before. I've never *wanted* to put myself out there and be vulnerable to being turned down by a man. Thinking about Brady, I begin to feel that inexplicable pull toward him again. I feel like I *need* to go tonight and see where this goes.

Taking a deep breath, I reply to my brother.

Me: *I'll see you at nine.*

At 9:07, I walk into Rick's. Riser is on stage already, singing a song I love but can never remember the name of. I'm horrible at remembering titles of songs.

Teresa sees me and waves me over, so I head to their table. There aren't as many people with them as last time, but two other couples are sitting with them. We all say hi, then I take a seat next to Teresa. There's an empty chair on the other side of me, and I idly wonder if Brady will be here soon.

"You look great, Kelsey," Teresa says. "I love your outfit!"

"Thanks," I reply, looking down at the casual jeans, blouse, and boots I have on. Her compliment makes me smile because I have to admit, I tried my best to look good tonight.

Nolan, Teresa, their friends, and I make small talk and listen to the band. I order a Pepsi and try to relax. By 9:50, I begin to wonder when Brady will actually get here.

As if he read my mind again, Nolan leans over and says, so only I can hear, "Brady should be here soon. He got off work at nine."

Trying not to react to my brother the way I'm feeling inside—aka jumping up and down with excitement—I look at him and raise an eyebrow. "What makes you think that matters to me?"

Nolan chuckles. "I'm your brother. I can tell." He winks at me, then takes a swig of his drink and turns his attention back to Riser.

I shake my head, still trying to act nonchalant, and then my eye happens to catch Brady walking in the door.

Holy hell, he looks delicious.

I quickly turn back to the band on stage, hoping my emotions aren't displayed all over my face. I rack my brain, trying to think of clever things to say to him and conversations we can have tonight. *Shit!* Time is running out—he'll be at the table any second!

"Brady!" Nolan's voice booms, and I turn to see my brother standing, embracing Brady in a man-hug. I take a sip of my Pepsi to buy some time, trying to calm my nerves. They let each other go, and Nolan invites Brady to sit in the one empty chair at the table next to me.

As Brady takes a seat, I get a whiff of his cologne. The scent is just as good as I remember, and it puts all my senses on full alert. As casually as I possibly can, I turn to Brady and smile.

His mouth turns up and his dimples pop; his blue eyes sparkle in the dim lighting of the bar. "Hi, Kelsey," he says, his deep, sexy voice sounding smooth as caramel.

"Hi," I reply, my voice sounding more breathy than I intend. Was that sexy? Or just weird? I begin to doubt myself, but when Brady's smile widens, I know I don't need to worry.

"How are you? I've been so busy at work. I wish we could've hung out more over the past few months."

Did he really just say that? I try not to let my jaw hit the table and don't let my facial expressions show just how giddy I'm feeling at the moment. *He wanted to hang out with me?*

I don't know what to say, but Brady continues before I can

35

respond. "I mean, we're practically neighbors. I should've at least dropped by to borrow a cup of sugar or something."

Brady smirks at me, and my insides practically melt. I am so damned attracted to this man that I don't even know what to do with myself or what to say. I need to get a grip and act cool; otherwise, he's going to be completely turned off.

I'm saved by the band, though, as they finish the song they were playing, and everyone in the bar erupts in cheers. Turning our attention to the stage, we clap. I'm grateful for the extra few seconds it gives me to get a hold of myself. Once Riser starts playing the next song, I turn toward Brady again.

"So you just got off work?" I ask him, hoping this strikes up a conversation that will easily lead to other topics so we can get to know each other a little better.

He nods. "Yeah, it was a slow night. I wanted to leave earlier, but we're already shorthanded in the department, so I had to stay in case something came up. Nothing did, though, so I was able to get off on time. I was looking forward to coming here tonight." Brady smiles again, and I get the feeling he's trying to tell me something … maybe that he was looking forward to seeing me?

I can only hope.

"Me, too," I say, keeping the conversation rolling. "When Nolan texted me about coming tonight, I knew it was exactly what I needed after a long week at work."

"Same here, except my week isn't over yet. I work tomorrow and Sunday, too."

I raise my eyebrows, surprised to find out he works weekends. I don't know why that surprises me, but it does. "Oh, you don't have weekends off?" I ask, wondering what his schedule is.

He shakes his head. "No, unfortunately being the ex-chief's son doesn't pull any weight in getting the good days off," he says with a chuckle. "I work Thursday through Sundays, eleven to nine. We work four tens, so at least I get three-day weekends. My weekends just fall on Mondays, Tuesdays, and Wednesdays."

I nod in understanding. "I see. Do you like that schedule?"

Brady shrugs his shoulders. "Eh, it has its benefits. Most people work on my days off, so if I want to go anywhere, it's never very crowded. It just sucks when my friends want to get together on the weekends. I don't usually go out when I have to work the next day, but I made an exception since Nolan said you'd be here."

Oh. His comment makes my insides twist and turn, but in a good way. I smile, and he smiles back. God, he makes me want to lean in and kiss him ... but I know this would not be a good time for that. Knowing that he came here just to see me gives me a feeling I've never felt before. I'm at a loss for words as I admire Brady's good-looking features; his slightly messy brown hair, the stubble on his face that only seems to make him sexier, and even how straight his teeth are. I can't remember if he had braces when he was younger.

"I'm really glad to see you again," Brady says, pulling me out of my inner thoughts. His words warm my soul, and I realize I need to let him know I feel the same way.

"Well, that's good to hear," I tell him. Luckily, my voice doesn't shake with all the nerves I'm feeling. "I have to admit, I was excited when Nolan told me you'd be here tonight. It's really good to see you again, too."

Just then, a waitress approaches us and asks if we need anything. With my Pepsi still half full, I decline, but Brady orders a beer. After she disappears to get his drink, Brady asks, "Do you ever drink alcohol?"

Crap. I guess he doesn't know I'm fifteen years sober and proud of it. I wonder what he'll think of this. "No, I never do. I kind of can't."

Brady looks apologetic as if he just remembered that I was an addict in high school. "Shit. I hope that didn't sound rude! I didn't mean for it to sound that way."

His thoughtfulness makes me smile. "No, I didn't take it that way at all. I've gotten used to the question over the years."

He looks relieved, then curious again. "Do you mind me asking why you can't drink? Have you just sworn off all substances?"

I take a breath before answering. "I've been sober since I was seventeen years old. I don't drink, smoke, or do any drugs. Not even marijuana even though it's legal now. If you ever need a designated driver, I'm the one to call." I wink, letting him know I added that last part as a joke.

Brady smiles shyly, and I can tell he either feels uncomfortable with this conversation, or he's embarrassed he brought it up. He knows the short and sweet version of my story from our brief conversation at Nolan's on the Fourth of July, and I really don't want to dive back into that right now.

"You're pretty amazing, Kelsey," he says, taking me by surprise. I really didn't expect those to be his next words, and I'm flattered.

I nervously look away from him and fidget with the straw in my glass. "Thank you," I reply, unsure of what else to say.

"It sounds like you went through a lot when you were younger," he continues, and I force myself to look into his eyes again. "You should be proud of who you've become, and how strong you obviously are. I'm in awe of you."

Everything around me seems to disappear. It's as if Brady and I are alone, and he's all I see. If I didn't already feel a strong attraction to this man, now it's ten times stronger.

Brady and I stare into each other's eyes, and I feel that electric pull toward him again. I know, at this moment, I'm exactly where I'm supposed to be.

When the waitress's arm breaks our eye contact, I'm brought back to reality. She places Brady's beer on the table, and we both look up at her. "Thank you," he says before she asks if she can get us anything else. We politely tell her no, and then she walks away again.

Brady and I look at one another again, and his kind smile lets me know that he likes me. A sense of calm washes over me. I want to know everything there is to know about Brady Danner, and I hope to learn a little more tonight.

As the saying goes, time flies when you're having fun. Brady and I spend the evening talking and getting to know each other, while also having side conversations with Nolan and Teresa. Before I know it, it's after midnight, and my brother announces that he and Teresa are heading home. Then their other friends decide to leave, too. Brady glances at his watch, and says, "It's getting late."

Like the last time we were at Rick's, I suddenly wonder what'll happen next. Will we just hug again? Will we kiss this time? Will this lead to more between us? We learned a little about each other tonight. He studied finance in college, only to end up going into law enforcement. He also went to school on a baseball scholarship, joined a fraternity, and was once engaged to his college sweetheart. She broke off the engagement, though, so he has never married.

I told him about my college years even though mine weren't nearly as exciting. We also learned we have a lot in common— from the type of music we listen to, to the food we like, to the movies and TV shows we enjoy watching.

As everyone around us gets up to leave, Brady and I stand to say goodbye to them all. When I hug Teresa, she says in my ear, "Have fun with Brady tonight!"

I shake my head, and reply, "He's just a friend!" No need to get them excited over something that I'm not even sure is happening yet! But I happen to notice Nolan saying something to Brady as well, and I know this is out of my hands now. My brother and his wife are going to be all up in my business tomorrow, asking what happened between Brady and me after they left.

Once everyone else at our table has gone, Brady turns to me, and says, "I hate to end this, but I really should get home soon. If I didn't have to work tomorrow, I'd stay out all night with you. I'm really enjoying our time together."

Although I feel let down that our night is about to end, I also understand. "That's okay," I reply. "Maybe we can get together again sometime."

Brady smiles as he says, "I'd love that."

He walks me to my car, and as much as I'm dreading being a disappointment, I can only hope that Brady kisses me tonight. I want to feel his lips on mine. I've enjoyed getting to know him better, and I couldn't be more attracted to him if I tried. I want to know what it's like to be kissed for real ... by someone who genuinely likes me, and who seems to have the same feelings for me that I have for him.

"Thanks for tonight," he says, taking a step closer to me as we stand next to my car in the parking lot. His hands reach for my waist, and when he touches me, I swear I feel sparks.

"I had a good time," I reply, unsure of what else to say.

Brady just looks at me for a moment before he adds, "Let's not wait three months to hang out together again."

I'm tongue-tied, and I feel like an idiot. All I can do is smile and let out a quiet giggle.

"Kelsey," he starts to say, and he moves a fraction closer to me. Before I know it, he lowers his head closer to mine, and I know it's coming; he's going to kiss me. Panic wells up in me, and I pray to God my kissing skills are up to par. Tonight has been perfect, and I don't want to ruin it by not knowing how to properly kiss the man good night.

Slowly, his lips brush over mine, and I try to contain myself. This kiss is everything I could wish it to be. We move together as if we've kissed a million times before, and I'm surprised to find that I'm actually good at this! It may have been years since I kissed a man, but it's like riding a bicycle. I worried for nothing.

In fact, it's better than I remember it ever being before. Maybe it's just the fact it's Brady.

Our lips move sensually together, and my arms move around his waist. He pulls me closer to him, then his tongue swipes my lips. I open my mouth, and his tongue finds mine. His strong hands stroke my back slowly, and it feels like I'm floating in a dream.

Unexpectedly, he pulls away from me, leaving me wondering if he regrets kissing me. "Sorry," he says, combing his hand through his hair, leaving it slightly messier than it already was. I can't help but find the messy look on Brady sexy.

"For what?" I ask, hoping he doesn't regret what's happened between us. I really like him.

"I'm not sure if I'm moving too fast for you," he says, and I can tell he's nervous to hear my response.

I shake my head. "No. I enjoyed that kiss."

His lips curve into a smile, and he moves closer to me, putting his hands on my hips. "I did, too," he says before crashing his lips to mine once more.

I melt into him, placing my hands on his upper arms as we passionately kiss again. It's as if his lips fit perfectly with mine. We move in sync, and I can't help but let out a quiet moan. I'm enjoying this kiss so much. It seems to go on forever, and I don't want it to end, but then it does.

Brady rests his forehead against mine, and says, "I really like you, Kelsey."

I smile. "I like you, too."

"I'll call you tomorrow," he says, then kisses my forehead and pulls away again. This time, he pulls his phone out of his pocket and asks for my number. I give it to him, then he sends me a text so I have his number, too.

"Have a good night, Kelsey. Drive safe home," he says.

"You, too, Brady," I reply, smiling at him. Then turns and walks away.

KELSEY

*a*s I drive home and come down from what I can only describe as a high from Brady Danner, I analyze my feelings. I've never felt this way before. What is it about Brady that I can't resist? He's my brother's friend, not to mention the son of the man who arrested me as a teenager. Sure, I've totally turned my life around since then, but the irony that I am having these feelings for a cop is not lost on me. I spent my teenage years avoiding cops like the plague.

I notice Brady's car following me all the way home. Well, of course he's right behind me, considering he lives in the same complex. It warms my heart when I think about how he told me to drive safe, yet he's right behind me like the protector he is.

After I park in my spot, I see Brady's car continue to drive toward his building farther back in the complex. I touch my lips, remembering how amazing it felt to kiss him. I hope I get to kiss him again soon.

As I unlock my front door, I can't help but wonder how Brady really feels about me. He says he likes me, and I can tell he does by the way he kissed me, but I still wonder what he thinks of me. Maybe he just likes to have fun with women, and I'm his newest conquest. With his good looks, I'm sure he could have his pick of women. What is it about me that he likes? Sure, we have a lot in common, but we've also lived very different lives. My past is beyond questionable, especially for a cop.

The thought depresses me as I let myself into my apartment and set my keys and purse down. I plop onto my couch and let out a sigh. Closing my eyes, I let my mind wander. I can't help but imagine being in Brady's arms again, looking into his blue eyes and feeling his lips pressed against mine.

Brady makes me feel things I'm not accustomed to. I can't help it when my hand slides down my belly to the waistband of my jeans … even though I wish it was Brady's hand and not mine. I slide it into my pants, under my panties, letting my mind take me to a place it hasn't gone in so long …

And then there's a knock on my door.

Startled, I yank my hand out of my pants as my eyes fly open. Who the hell is knocking on my door at this hour? *Fuck!*

"Kelsey, it's Brady," I hear him say from the other side of the door.

Oh, my God. *What is he doing here?*

I realize I need to do something. I stand and cross the floor to the entryway, hesitant to reach for the door handle. Why is he here? What does this mean?

He knocks again. "Kelsey, open up," he says. His voice sounds soft but with a little authority behind it.

I take a deep breath and steady myself as I open the door.

"Hi," he says, a tentative smile forming on his lips. His hands are in his pockets, and he looks unsure of himself, as if he doesn't quite know why he's here either. But he also looks delicious, and I can't help but smile back. My heart is beating so hard, I'm sure he can hear it.

"Hi," I reply, my voice almost a whisper. We stand looking at each other for a moment before I finally get the nerve to ask him to come inside.

Brady steps toward me, and at least I have enough wits about myself to move aside so he can come in. As he passes me, I get a whiff of his cologne, and I'm again turned on even more than I was before. Everything about Brady Danner is just so ... amazing.

I can't help but gawk as he strides across my living room toward the couch. Closing the front door, I say, "Have a seat."

"Thanks," he replies. He really looks more nervous than I've ever seen him.

I sit on the opposite end of the couch, bending my knee so I can face him. "What brings you here?" I ask.

Brady chuckles as he rubs his chin with his hand. Then he stops, and when he looks into my eyes, he takes my breath away with his sexiness. "Honestly, I don't know. After we left the bar, I wanted to see you again ... so here I am."

"Oh," I reply, smiling at him.

"Kelsey," Brady says, sitting up and leaning his elbows on his knees. "I enjoyed getting to know you better tonight, but I want to know more about you. I didn't want to say good night when we left."

My heart pounds harder, and I feel my cheeks start to blush. Just a few moments ago, I was fantasizing about Brady, and now he's here, telling me he wants to know me better.

"When we kissed, I felt as if we have good chemistry," he continues, looking nervous as he looks at me with sincerity in his eyes. "Was I correct in feeling that way?"

I swallow, unsure of how to carry on this conversation when all I want to do is jump onto Brady's lap and kiss the hell out of him.

Noticing Brady's uncertainty, I suddenly want him to know he was not imagining the chemistry between us. So I boldly do something I've never done before; I make a move.

Taking a deep breath, I move closer to Brady. "You're right. I felt the same way."

He looks at me, and his lips curve into a smile. "Good," he

replies as he, too, moves closer to me. Before I know it, Brady's hands are cupping my face, his eyes looking into mine with an emotion I've never experienced before. I swear my heart skips a beat. Brady leans in closer, and then his lips are covering mine.

It's a slow and tender kiss. My eyes close, and I let myself enjoy this moment. My hands instinctively wrap around Brady's waist. Before I know it, I'm lying on my back with Brady on top of me. His hands gently stroke my face and my hair. His body covers mine, and it feels heavenly. He grinds his hips into mine, and I can feel his rather large bulge, making me want more of him. My hands stroke his back, the back of his head, and his arms as our kiss becomes more desperate. I can't get enough of Brady.

Just as I'm enjoying all the sensations he's giving me, his hand makes its way up my shirt. At first, I enjoy his hand touching my skin … but as he gets closer to my breast, I begin to feel claustrophobic and panicked, even. I can't help myself when I push his hand and pull my lips away, telling him to get off me.

Brady immediately does as I ask, and we both sit up. *Holy shit.* What just happened? I was enjoying everything about Brady, so why did I have to freak out? I look at Brady, and he's obviously confused, but I can tell he's also concerned.

"Are you okay?" he asks. "Did I hurt you?"

I shake my head as embarrassment wells up inside me. I lean over with my elbows on my knees and cover my face with my hands. I feel Brady's hand on my back as he rubs it up and down, trying to soothe me.

"What happened?" he asks, his voice calm and gentle, letting me know he's safe and he cares. The irony is, I *do* feel safe with him, so why did I have to go and have that reaction when he touched me?

Taking a deep breath, I lift my head and turn to look at him. He stops rubbing my back and gives me his full attention. I know I can trust him, and I know he cares. I shouldn't have anything to worry about when it comes to telling Brady my secrets. I don't know *how* I know all this, but I do. However, looking into his calm blue eyes, I just can't bring myself to tell him the truth.

"I ... I just haven't been with a man in a long time," I lie. Although it really is true—I haven't been with a man in years— it's just not the real reason for my freak-out.

"So you're nervous?" Brady places his hand on my knee gently. His touch doesn't bother me now, and I wish we could go back to where we were before I reacted so badly.

I nod. "Yes and no. You don't make me nervous, but I'm nervous that I won't live up to your expectations." While this is embarrassingly true, it's still easier to discuss right now than what's really wrong with me.

Brady visibly calms as his shoulders relax. "Kelsey, you don't have anything to worry about. I think you're amazing."

"Thanks," I say although it comes out as a whisper. His response actually chokes me up. He thinks I'm amazing? No one has ever told me that before.

"We'll take things slow," he says, giving my knee a squeeze. "I don't want to make any mistakes with you."

Is this really happening? Brady is the most understanding man I've ever met, aside from my dad and brother. I hold back my tears and have to look away from him for a moment to gain my composure.

"I'll call you tomorrow," Brady says as he stands. I look up at him, not wanting him to leave, but I know it's the best thing right now. There's no recovering from what just happened. I need to get a grip on my past issues so this doesn't happen again.

I stand, and he takes one of my hands in his. I love the way his hand feels wrapped around mine. It feels strong, warm, and safe.

"Good night," he says, then leans in and kisses me gently on the lips. Only this time, it's just a quick kiss before he pulls away again.

He lets go of my hand and walks toward the door. I follow

him, wishing things had gone differently tonight. We should still be kissing, or more.

Brady opens the door but turns to me before leaving. "Bye, Kelsey," he says, planting another kiss on my forehead.

"Bye," I reply before he turns and walks out the door. I close the door behind him, then slump down to the floor.

I burst into tears. I can't explain it. I just need to cry it out.

BRADY

What the fuck just happened?

As I walk back to my apartment, I wonder what caused Kelsey's reaction. It has to be more than just being nervous. She acted as if she was having a flashback, like I triggered something by touching her under her shirt. I know she made bad choices when she was younger, but now I'm thinking there's more she's not telling me.

Tonight was amazing. I finally got the chance to spend time with Kelsey again. Three months is a long time to wait, and I'm kicking myself for not making a move sooner. I really have no excuse other than working too much. Even though I'm working in a small town now, it doesn't make my days any shorter or less tiring. It's just a different sort of tired. Instead of dealing with big city gang members, homeless people who need mental health assistance, and the fear of being attacked and either hurt or killed on the job, I'm dealing with a lot of domestic disputes. Most of them are ridiculous calls, and I end up basically helping adults solve their problems like children. It gets even more interesting when they're drunk, which is usually the case. Once in a while, it's more serious, where punches have been thrown and a woman or child has been hurt. Those are the worst. I can't get those calls out of my head, and they leave me mentally exhausted.

But excuses aside, I should've made an effort to see Kelsey again before now. I was grateful when Nolan texted me earlier, telling me some people were meeting at Rick's to see Riser again. When he mentioned Kelsey would be there, I knew I had to go even though I had to work tomorrow. I couldn't wait any longer to spend time with her.

Everything was great … until it wasn't. I feel terrible for making her pull away. I know now that I need to be careful with Kelsey and take things slow. She obviously has something haunting her that she's not ready to tell me about yet.

I can't explain why I feel so strongly for Kelsey. We've only hung out a few times, and while we have a lot in common, I feel as if my feelings are too strong, too soon. She's beautiful, and I was attracted to her the moment I laid eyes on her at Nolan's house. After we spent time together at Rick's the first time, I knew she was special. I felt an inexplicable pull toward her as though I *had* to get to know her better. No, like I was *meant* to get to know her better. It might sound crazy, but that was how I felt back then.

Tonight just solidified my feelings for her. I could've kept talking to her all night. I want to know everything about her and spend more time with her. And when we kissed … it was even more amazing than I thought it would be. Our lips fit together perfectly, and kissing her took my breath away.

I know she's Nolan's sister, but I also know he's cool with me dating her. After all, he's the one who tried to set us up. It's funny how I never paid attention to her when we were growing up. She was just Nolan's little sister. I never thought of her as pretty or anything; in fact, I never think about her at all. But when I looked back at our senior yearbook last summer and saw her sophomore picture, I saw just how beautiful she was back then. How did I not notice her? I guess it was just because she was my friend's sister, plus she was two years younger than us. Two years is a big difference at that age, which seems kind of funny now.

As I crawl into my bed, I can't get Kelsey off my mind. I hope she's okay. It pains me to think that I did something to make her pull away. What has she been through? I care about Kelsey, and I hope I can help her get through this.

The next morning, I wake to the sound of my alarm going off. As I shut it off, Kelsey is at the forefront of my mind again. It's 9:15, so I need to get up and get ready for work, but I decide to send her a quick text to let her know I'm thinking about her.

Me: *Good morning, beautiful. I hope you have a good day.*

After I shower, I check my phone to see what time it is ... and to see if Kelsey replied yet. I smile as soon as I see she did.

Kelsey: *Good morning, handsome. I hope you have a good day, too.*

Okay, then. Texting dialogue seems good so far. She must be feeling better this morning. I decide to text her again.

Me: *I'd love to talk to you later. Can I call if I get a chance while I'm at work?*

. . .

I set my phone down and slather shaving cream on my face. Just as I'm about to start shaving, my phone dings with a text. I set the razor down and look at my phone again.

Kelsey: *You can call me any time.*

Again, her response makes me smile. I send her a smiley face emoji, then go about finishing my morning routine.

Though work has been busy today, I finally hit a lull sometime around four o'clock. I decide to pull into the high school parking lot for my break. I'm starving, so I open my lunch bag and take out a protein bar to eat. I also take my personal phone out and pull up Kelsey's number. I've been wanting to hear her voice, and now I finally seem to have the time to do it, so I take the chance.

The phone rings three times before she answers. "Hi there," her soft, kind voice answers, instantly making me smile.

"Hi," I reply. "How are you?"

"I'm good. How are you?"

"I'm doing pretty well myself. I finally got some downtime today, so I thought I'd give you a call. What are you up to?"

Kelsey sighs as if she's been busy. "I've been doing laundry and cleaning all day. Exciting stuff," she says with a little laugh.

I love the sound of her voice. It has a soothing quality to it, and I feel myself relax as we continue to talk about household chores. It occurs to me that this is what's happened every time I've been around Kelsey in person, too. Even when we briefly bumped into each other the few times in the past three months, as soon I'd see her, I'd feel instantly calm. Nothing, or no one, has ever had this effect on me before, and the realization makes me like her even more.

I need to see her again.

"What are you doing later tonight?" I ask after we finish our conversation about which laundry detergent we each prefer.

Jesus, were we really just talking about detergent?

"Um, nothing," she replies. "Why?" She sounds hopeful, as if she wants to see me again, too. At least, I hope that's what she wants.

"I want to see you again. I don't get off work until nine, so it'll be late, though. Would you want to get together around ten?"

"Sure," she says, then adds, "Why don't you just come over to my apartment?"

"Sounds like a plan," I reply, glad she wants to see me as well. I hope to God that I don't get any late calls tonight that keep me working later than nine.

And with that thought, a call comes through on my radio.

"Sorry, I have to go," I say to Kelsey. We say our goodbyes, and I get back to work.

It's Saturday night, and God didn't grant my wish. I should've known better than to make plans after work on a weekend. Even in Tenino, people like to party it up, and while it's not as busy and crazy as in Portland, there also aren't as many of us cops to handle all the disturbance calls. Long story short, I don't clock out at the precinct until almost eleven o'clock.

As soon as I knew I was going to be late, I texted Kelsey to let her know. Luckily, she understood. I've actually dated women in the past who got mad at me for having to work late. As if I could just tell my boss I had a date and have to leave. Ha! I don't know what world those women lived in, but Kelsey seems more down to earth.

When I get in my car to drive home, I text her again to let her know I'm finally leaving, but I need to stop at home first to shower. I'm exhausted and don't exactly smell or look my best after this twelve-hour day. I also tell her I understand if she's tired and wants to take a rain check since I won't get to her place until midnight.

Kelsey: *Can you come over tomorrow instead? I'm falling asleep. :(*

Me: *Of course. Hopefully, it won't be so busy and I can get off on time. I'm so sorry about tonight.*

Kelsey: *Stop apologizing. I totally understand! I hope you get a good night's sleep, and I look forward to seeing you tomorrow.*

Me: *Thank you for being so understanding. I can't wait to see you tomorrow.*

Kelsey: *Neither can I.*

With that, I set my phone down and drive home, thinking of Kelsey with a smile on my face the whole way.

KELSEY

Sunday nights are usually a little depressing, having to think about going to work the next day. Even though I love my job, I don't know anyone who enjoys the thought of the weekend ending. However, tonight I'm not depressed or thinking about work at all; tonight, Brady's coming over, and I can't wait to see him again.

Yes, I'm nervous as hell and don't know what to expect. Yes, I'm freaked out that I'll have the same reaction if we start making out again. But I came to a realization this weekend: I finally have feelings for a man—a good, decent man—and I need to work through whatever bad feelings came back to me the other night if I ever want to have a healthy, happy relationship. And that's exactly what I'd like to have with Brady. For the first time in my life, I want this.

Brady texts me a few times throughout the day, letting me know he's thinking about me and updating me on his workday. Luckily, it turns out to be a slow night for him, and when he texts me at 9:04 saying he's on his way home, I instantly smile. Butterflies pick up in my belly at the thought of seeing him in about an hour, but I can't wait until he gets here.

At 10:01, there's a knock on my door. I take a deep breath to steady my nerves as I head to my front door. When I open it and see Brady standing there, wearing a Rainier Renegades hoodie— the Tacoma football team who is predicted to make it to the Super Bowl this year—and his hair slightly messed up and looking sexy as ever, a wide smile crosses my face.

He smiles back, and I feel a shiver run through my body. This man is handsome as hell, but when he smiles, those dimples pop and his face lights up, amplifying his good looks by a thousand. To think he's smiling just because of me also makes me feel things I've never felt before.

"Hi," he says, and I realize I'm just staring at him.

"Hi. Come on in," I reply, moving aside so he can enter. I close the door, and we settle on the couch, just as we did a couple of nights ago.

"How was work?" I ask even though I pretty much already know the answer from his various texts throughout the day.

"Good. Not too busy." He looks apologetic all of a sudden, as if something just occurred to him. "Crap, you have to work tomorrow. I don't want to keep you up late."

"It's okay," I tell him because it's the truth. "I usually don't go to bed until around eleven, even on school nights. I'm a night owl."

"You and I have that in common. Like a lot of other things," Brady says with a chuckle.

"That's true," I reply. "We really do have a lot in common." I smile at him and wonder where this conversation is going. I'd been looking forward to seeing him all day, but I didn't know what to expect.

"It's nice when you find someone easy to talk to. I really enjoy the conversations we have, Kelsey."

"Me, too."

"I've been thinking about you a lot," Brady adds. He leans

forward and places his elbows on his knees. "I'm concerned about what happened the other night."

I knew he was going to bring this up. It was too much to hope I'd luck out and be able to avoid it.

Looking at my hands in my lap, I think about what I want to say to him. While I've thought about what to tell him a lot over the past forty-eight hours, I never came to any clear conclusions. I could be totally honest and candid, but that might scare him away. Or I could tell him half-truths and hope he doesn't freak out. Or I could lie and make excuses for my behavior. Now that I'm facing the situation head on, I still don't know what to do. My heart rate picks up, and my palms get sweaty.

"It's okay," he continues. "You can tell me anything."

I look at him and see how sincere he's being. I really do feel that I can trust him, but my past isn't something I'm always comfortable telling people. I take a breath and make my decision. Half-truths will do for now.

"The thing is," I begin, looking back at my hands. It's hard to look someone in the eye when I tell this story. "I already told you I did a lot of drugs in high school. I'm not proud of the things I did, but I can't change them now. I told you I was addicted to heroin …" I look at Brady again to gauge his reaction. He nods in understanding, and then I continue. "My first sexual experiences weren't exactly normal." Looking back at my hands, I rub them together, hoping Brady can accept what I'm going to tell him. It may not be the whole truth, but his reaction will determine if I tell him more in the future.

"Kelsey," Brady says, and I look back at him again. "This happened years ago. You've changed a lot since then, and I know you're not the same person you were in high school. Whatever you have to tell me, I'm not going to judge you."

"Well, for one, I don't remember losing my virginity," I begin, cringing as I watch for his reaction. "I was drunk and don't remember a thing about the experience."

"Okay …" he says, and I can tell he's trying not to express his mortification. "I'm sorry that's how it happened for you." Brady pauses and rubs the back of his neck. I wonder what's going through his mind. After a moment, he looks at me and relaxes back into the couch. "If it makes you feel any better, my first time sucked, too."

My eyebrows raise in surprise, and I try my best to relax as well. "Is that right?" I ask, prompting him to go on. Although I know it can't compare to my train wreck, I'm curious what made his first time bad.

He chuckles. "Well, for starters, it was my freshman year of college, and I basically did it just to get it over with. I felt like the last virgin on campus, but I didn't have a girlfriend, so I slept with this girl who all the guys seemed to know …" He gives me a pointed look. "You know what I mean … she got around, and we really meant nothing to each other. But I did it, and that was it. A few months later, I met a girl I ended up dating for a long time. I wish I had lost my virginity to her instead, since her first time was actually with me." Brady shrugs, looking a little sad at the memory. "Oh well. You can't change the past. You just have to move on."

"Well, that's for sure," I reply. "I know all too well how to move on from bad choices in my past."

"So I guess both our first times were rough," Brady says. "But that still doesn't explain why you pushed me away Friday night." He leans closer to me, placing his hand on my knee and looking me in the eye. "I care about you, Kelsey, and I want to avoid hurting you like that again. Please tell me what happened."

I briefly close my eyes and wish things could be different. Brady is the most understanding man I've ever met, but I still can't be completely honest with him about this. I know he would look at me differently. He may not even want to touch me again.

Opening my eyes, I place my hand on top of his, still resting on my knee. I decide to give him a little more insight without telling him everything. "Let's just say sex has never been one hundred percent positive experiences for me. I guess when you touched my bare skin, it subconsciously triggered one of my bad experiences. I can't explain it; in fact, I can't even recall what the bad experience was. I don't remember a lot. I just suddenly felt …" I search for the right word to use, not wanting to insult or scare him in some way. "Brady, I was enjoying myself with you. I felt safe, it was a good experience, and I was totally turned on by you. I wanted to keep going and do more, so please don't think I didn't. I guess I just felt insecure and worried that this would somehow turn out like all the other times. I've never had good sex, and I don't have a lot of experience."

Brady squeezes my knee and looks at me with sadness in his eyes, but understanding written all over his face. It only makes me like him more, and I also feel terrible for not being completely honest with him.

"Kelsey, you have nothing to worry about with me. I'm sorry you haven't had good sexual experiences in your life. I haven't had a lot of partners either, if that helps. What I've learned, though, is that it doesn't matter how much experience you have; it's how you and your partner work together to make it good."

I look at Brady and let his words sink in. I hope he's right. Maybe things *can* be different with him.

"I want you to know we can take things as slow as you want. I'm not in a hurry. I like you, Kelsey, and I just want to get to know you better."

His words make me smile. He really is a good man, and I feel honored that he actually likes me. "Thank you, Brady. I really appreciate that. And I also want to get to know you better."

We look at each other, not saying a word, but it's as if we're communicating something. I can't explain this feeling I have for Brady; it's so unlike anything I've felt before, and I have to admit, it scares me a little.

Brady looks at his watch, breaking our eye contact. "It's late. I should go so you can get some rest before tomorrow."

Though I feel a little let down that he's leaving so soon, I try not to let it show. "Oh, okay. I'm glad you came over, though."

"Me, too," he replies, then stands.

I walk him to the door, but when we get there, he takes me by surprise. Brady turns, steps closer to me, then places his hands on the side of my face, and kisses me. After the initial shock wears off, I melt into him, my hands gripping his arms. But just as I think this kiss won't end, it does. Brady pulls his lips away, resting his forehead against mine. "I'll call you tomorrow. I want to see you again soon." He kisses my forehead, then turns to leave.

"I want to see you again, too," I say as he starts to open the door.

He looks back at me, smiling. "I'm so glad. See you later, Kelsey."

Brady leaves, closing the door behind him, and I feel as if I've just won the lottery. I can't wipe the smile off my face, and I feel energized. It's late, though, and I have to work in the morning, so I lock my front door and go to bed with Brady on my mind.

The next day, Brady and I text each other throughout the day. He has the day off, so he's at home. Getting texts from him while I'm at work makes me feel good. It also makes my day go by faster. He invites me out to dinner tonight, and I accept. I'm on cloud nine and so excited for our date tonight.

Just before school is out for the day, Bridget comes to see me. She looks pissed off as she slumps into my office and sits on the chair across from me, slouching and crossing her arms.

"What's up, Bridget?" I ask, curious to what brings her into my office this time. I can tell this girl is crying for help from me since she does this at least twice a week. Sometimes, she tells me what's bothering her, and other times, she just beats around the bush until it's time to go home. I haven't quite figured her out yet, except for the fact that she reminds me of myself at that age, and I know she needs me.

"Beacher kicked me out of class," she says, rolling her eyes, referring to her biology teacher.

"Why?"

"I don't know." I look at her, cocking an eyebrow as if to say *I'm not dumb,* and she takes a deep breath before continuing. "He put me on the spot again. I couldn't remember all the steps of the cell cycle. He made me feel stupid in front of everyone, so I refused to talk anymore. He got mad and told me to leave. So here I am."

I raise my eyebrows to let her know I'm surprised at her behavior even though I'm really not. And, honestly, I don't really blame her for doing what she did. Beacher has been teaching at Yelm since before I was ever a student here, and he's old school. He thinks embarrassing kids will miraculously turn their study skills around. I know this because I was once in his class, and he did the same to me. If I was his boss, I'd have some choice words with the guy, but that's not my job.

"Well, Bridget, I'm sorry he put you on the spot. I can understand why you felt the way you did. However, do you think you could have handled the situation better?" Even though I disagree with the teacher in this case, it's still my job as the school counselor to help kids work through their problems in a respectful, mature way, and shutting down and refusing to speak to a teacher is not respectful or mature.

Bridget shrugs her shoulders, not answering me right away, so I wait her out. I can tell she's mulling things over in her head, and I hope she doesn't shut down on me as well. Finally, after a couple of minutes, she does speak. "I guess I could've just told him I didn't do my homework and don't know the answer."

"That's a start," I reply, glad she's talking to me.

"But then he would've given me detention," she continues, "or said something else condescending and embarrassing."

I knit my eyebrows together, curious to what she means. "Condescending and embarrassing?" I ask, hoping she tells me something I can tell the administration about. I'd love to see Beacher be put in his place.

Bridget rolls her eyes again. "I don't know ... you know how he can be. He's just a jerk."

Well, that's not good enough evidence to take to my admin. *Damn.* "Well, Bridget, you may not have gotten detention, but you landed here in my office, and you're missing the end of class. Do you think that's going to help you learn the cell cycle and do well in bio? He probably reviewed it after you left the room."

Bridget considers what I said, and I can tell it occurs to her that what she did was foolish. "I guess you're right," she says, sulkily.

Then a thought occurs to me. "Bridget, did Beacher send you to my office? Or did you just come here on your own?"

She sits up a little in her chair and crosses her arms. "He didn't tell me where I had to go; he just kicked me out. So I came here."

A sense of pride wells up inside me. The fact she chose to come see me when her teacher kicked her out makes me feel good. I feel like I'm really starting to get through to this girl. She could have easily just left campus and gone who knows where, but she came to talk to me instead.

"I'm glad you came to talk to me," I tell her. "You're welcome in my office anytime, as long as I'm not in another meeting. I'm always here for you, Bridget."

Bridget actually cracks a smile, but it's only a fraction of a second before she realizes what she's doing and tries to cover it up. This girl is tough. "Thanks," she says.

"You're welcome. Now, tell me what you can do tonight to help yourself learn the cell cycle?"

She rolls her eyes, but then answers, "I can read the chapter in my bio book when I get home. Maybe google it, too."

"Good idea. Are you going to do it?"

She seems to contemplate her answer, but she finally says, "Yeah, I'll study tonight. We have a test in class tomorrow."

"Sounds like a plan," I reply, and I really hope she does it. According to her past grades, Bridget used to do well in school. Last year, things started to go downhill for her. I'm not sure what caused the shift, but like me, I'm sure it has to do with the friends she hangs out with.

Bridget stays in my office until the bell rings for school to be out. We don't talk about a whole lot, but she does share with me that her parents got divorced when she was twelve. Her dad left, and she hasn't seen him since then. My heart goes out to her, and I wonder if there's more going on with her home life that could be affecting her.

After she leaves, I finish some paperwork I need to do. Brady texts me again, and it immediately brings a smile to my face. He tells me he can't wait to see me in a couple of hours. I reply, telling him I'm looking forward to seeing him, too.

When I finally get home, I have an hour before Brady is due to pick me up for our date. I get myself ready, finding it nearly impossible to decide on an outfit. I have *never* been like this before! On the few dates I've been on, I never put so much thought into what I wore. I don't know what it is about Brady, but I just want to look nice for him.

At six o'clock sharp, there's a knock on my door. I check my reflection in the mirror one more time, satisfied with the outfit I finally chose, and then I head to the front door to answer it.

BRADY

*W*hen Kelsey opens her door, the sight of her takes my breath away. She's always beautiful, but she looks even more so tonight. I smile instantly and can't help but reach for her as I step inside her apartment. "Hi there," I say as my hands land on her hips, and I lower my mouth to hers. I can tell it takes her by surprise. I can't help myself, and I'm just glad she doesn't push me away. In fact, she wraps her arms around me and kisses me back.

We continue to kiss, and I take in all that I can. The floral scent of her perfume, which makes me want her more. The way her hands gently squeeze me as she holds me close. It's so subtle, she might not even realize she's doing it, but I notice. Everything about Kelsey has my attention in a good way. I like this woman a lot, and I've been looking forward to this date all day.

When we finally pull away from each other, my first instinct is to lean back in and kiss her again, but I control myself. Instead, I say, "You look beautiful. I mean, you're always beautiful, but you look especially nice tonight."

Kelsey smiles, blushes, and looks away. "Thank you," she says as she slips away from me and goes to grab her purse off the table. "You look nice, too," she adds as she walks back toward me.

"Thanks," I reply. When she reaches me again, I take her hand in mine. "Are you ready to go?"

She looks at me and smiles. "I am."

I drive us to Joanne Trattoria, the best Italian restaurant in town. It used to be the only Italian restaurant in town until a well-known chain opened its doors. While that place is good, and a lot of people are happy they opened in our small-but-growing town, I prefer to give my business to the local place that's been here for decades. Joanne's food is unbelievable, anyway.

Kelsey and I make small talk on the way to dinner, mostly about how much Yelm has changed over the years as we pass all the new developments. When we get to the restaurant, I'm happy we don't have to wait for a table. They don't take reservations; otherwise, I would've made one ahead of time, just in case it was busy. We're seated at a table in the corner, which is nice so we can talk without the other tables around us interrupting. I want to get to know Kelsey even more tonight. I want to know everything there is to know about her.

We quietly look at our menus, deciding on what we want to eat before diving into conversation. Or maybe we're just nervous. I don't know why, but I do feel a little nervous around Kelsey. I like her, a lot, and I want her to like me, too. However, I know I need to be careful with her because of what happened the other night. Even though she told me a little more about her past, I don't think she was totally honest about what caused her to push me away. I feel like she's still hiding something, but I also don't want to pressure her to tell me. I'll be patient with her and wait for her to tell me, but I hope she feels comfortable soon. I still feel horrible that I made her feel that way.

After the waiter takes our orders, I fold my hands on the table and look at Kelsey. I can't help the smile that forms on my face when I look at her, and I love that she smiles in return. We seem to have similar feelings for each other, and there's an inexplicable bond between us. I can't explain what it is, other than I feel a pull toward Kelsey that I've never felt toward a woman before.

"So tell me about your day at work," I start, deciding to start the conversation simple.

Kelsey tells me some of the highlights of her day, and I find myself drawn to her. Her job is so important, and she obviously has a passion for it. I admire her for that; for turning her life around and becoming a counselor to help other kids who struggle like she did. I see a lot of horrible things on the job, and she's on the other end of it, helping kids with the trauma they've been through or the bad choices they're making. It only makes me like her more.

Our conversation naturally switches to me, and I talk about my job. I tell her some of the highlights from the past few days as well as some of the more epic stories from years past. I definitely have more lively tales from my days in Portland. Tenino isn't nearly as exciting, but that's why I moved back to work there.

We continue talking through dinner. It's all very natural between us now; no nerves on my end, and I can tell that Kelsey has relaxed, too. The realization makes me happy, knowing that we're enjoying each other's company. I hope to get more nights like this with her.

A couple of hours later, we're still talking over coffee. Our dinner plates were cleared long ago, and we enjoyed sharing tiramisu for dessert. Our conversation just keeps going, flowing easily between us. We've covered so many topics tonight, and I've learned so much about Kelsey. Likewise, she's learned a lot about me. It's funny how all those years growing up, Kelsey was right there in front of me although *not* really there in front of me at the same time. Being one of my best friend's little sisters, I saw quite a bit of her around their house whenever I was over there; however, she never hung out with us, so I never got to know her back then. She was just there sometimes. After Nolan and I graduated, we went off to college and lost touch, and I never moved back to Yelm until now. It's funny how things turn out.

Kelsey takes a sip of her coffee, then glances at her watch after she sets her mug down. "Do you need to get home soon?" I ask, hoping the answer is no, but knowing she has to work tomorrow. I actually have no idea what time it is.

She shakes her head. "No, it's only eight thirty."

I smile, happy that I get more time with Kelsey. "Good. I'm really enjoying myself."

She smiles back, then says, "So am I. I'm so glad you asked me out, Brady."

Something about the way she says my name gets my attention in a way no one

else saying my name has before. It perks me up, and it's almost as if I feel static electricity in the air. It's a strange feeling, but I like it. I want to hear her say my name again and again.

By ten o'clock, the restaurant is shutting down, so we gather our things to leave. After being stuck with us for nearly four hours, the waiter definitely earned the hefty tip I left. I had the best time with Kelsey, though, and I don't want to go our separate ways. I know I'll have to take her home, though. She has to get up early for work tomorrow.

"Thank you so much for dinner," she says as we get in my car.

"You're so welcome," I reply. I start driving toward our apartment complex, and all of a sudden, I feel nervous again. How is our date going to end? Will she invite me in? If she does, will we talk, or do more than that? And if we do more, how far will we go this time? Hopefully, she doesn't get overwhelmed and push me away again. But if she does, I'll understand and be okay with it. I just hope we can eventually move past that if we're going to continue dating.

And I hope we do.

When we get to her apartment, I walk her to the door. "Would you like to come in?" she asks as she unlocks it.

"Sure, if you're okay with that," I reply. I want her to know that I'm going to let her take the lead here.

"I would love it if you came in for a bit," she says, opening the door. We walk in, and she closes the door behind us, locking the deadbolt. "Do you want anything to drink?"

"Water would be great," I reply, noticing my mouth is a little dry.

She walks into the kitchen and tells me to have a seat on the couch while she gets the water. I sit and look around her living room. She has a very nice home. Very comfortable and light. I like her decorating style, which is simple yet homey. Even though I've been in her house before, I never really paid that much attention. I really like her home.

Kelsey returns with two glasses of water and hands one to me. Then she sits next to me and takes a sip of her own water. After I take a sip of mine, I set the glass on the coffee table in front of me.

"I really like your home," I tell her.

"Thank you," she says, taking another sip of water. "It's pretty simple, but I like it here."

"I like the apartment complex, too, but I hope to buy a house in the next year or two," I tell her.

"That's an awesome goal. I'd love to buy a house someday, too, but I need to save more money for a down payment first."

"Same here," I reply. "I don't have that much saved up, unfortunately."

"Do you want to buy a house in Yelm? Or Tenino? Or somewhere else nearby?"

I rub my chin in thought. "I haven't actually given it that much thought yet. I guess it doesn't matter to me as long as I find a house I love. Although I probably won't buy a place in Tenino. It's nice to put a little distance between work and home."

"That makes sense," she says.

We continue talking for quite some time about various things.

I've learned so much about Kelsey tonight, it's scary to say, but I feel as if I'm falling in love with her.

Before we know it, our water glasses are empty, and it's nearly midnight.

"I should go home," I say although I don't really want to leave.

"Yeah, I guess it's getting late," she replies, looking a little sad that our night is ending. I wonder if she feels the same way I am.

"I've had an amazing time with you," I tell her, and I instinctively move closer to her, placing my hand on her knee. I can't help it; I just want to touch her and kiss her.

Kelsey looks at my hand on her knee, then up into my eyes. "I don't want you to go," she says, taking me completely by surprise. So I do the only logical thing I can, which is to lean in closer and kiss her. Hard.

This time, she doesn't push me away. My hands slowly and gently glide over her body, touching her everywhere—although I keep my hands *over* her clothing for now. Maybe if she warms up to my touch like this, it'll be easier for her to take the next step.

And she does, surprising me again. Her hands travel under my shirt, touching my skin, sending shivers through my body. As much as I want this, I want to make sure it's what Kelsey wants, so I pull my lips away just long enough to ask her, "Are you okay with this?"

"Yes," she answers between kisses. "I want you."

I don't waste another minute. Laying her down on the couch, I place my body over hers. Kissing her is like heaven. Touching her is amazing. And her hands on me feel incredible. I haven't been with a woman in a very long time, but that's not the only reason I'm feeling so much with Kelsey. I know I have strong feelings for her ... I think stronger than I've ever had for anyone else.

"Let's go to my room," she says. I stand and take her hand, helping her off the couch. As soon as she stands, I pull her to me and kiss her again. She starts walking toward her room, not breaking our kiss. I walk backward, letting her guide me to her bed. Once the back of my legs touch the mattress, I turn, still kissing her, and guide her onto the bed, crawling over her.

"You're so beautiful," I whisper as my lips kiss her neck. I feel her body shudder, and her hands wrap around my neck. She grips the back of my hair with one of her hands, which turns me on even more. She's obviously into it this time and not feeling the urge to push me away, so I'm grateful for that. I would definitely stop if she wanted me to, but I want her so badly, I'm hoping that won't happen.

I kiss my way down from her neck to her waist. She's still fully clothed, but I lift her shirt, exposing her belly. I kiss her hip, then kiss across to the other. I stop and look up at her to gauge her reaction. She looks completely turned on. Our eyes meet, and she rakes a hand through my hair. "Don't stop," she says.

"I just want to make sure you're okay," I say, then kiss her belly button before she can answer.

"You feel so good," Kelsey says, and I can hear the desire in her breathy voice.

I don't waste another minute. I move back up her body and kiss her mouth as my hand glides up her shirt. When I reach her bra, I dip my hand inside and moan when I touch her nipple. She moans as well, which turns me on even more.

God, she's sexy.

I need more of her. I sit up, pulling her up with me, and then I take her shirt off.

She looks gorgeous in her silky black bra. Kelsey surprises me again when she

reaches behind her back and unhooks her bra, sliding it off her shoulders and droppin

it to the floor. I can't contain myself and move back over her, kissing her neck, then

making my way down her smooth, soft skin to her bare breasts.

Gently, I lick her nipple, and her body writhes beneath me. "Oh," she whispers, and it's the sexiest sound I've ever heard. I keep going, licking, then sucking it into my mouth while simultaneously raking my hand over her skin, slowly letting it wander down to her belly.

I give Kelsey's other breast attention, and I nearly combust when she grips my hair again and lets out another moan. I need more of this woman; I don't know if I'll ever get enough of her.

My hand lazily makes its way under the waistband of her jeans and brushes her silky underwear. I wonder if her bra and panties match ... did she wear sexy underwear just for me? I have to know, so I move down her body again and undo her jeans. Feeling nervous all of a sudden, I realize how special this is; how lucky I am to be with Kelsey right now. She's the woman of my dreams, and for some reason, she likes me, too.

Pulling her jeans down her legs, I see in the dim light that yes, indeed, her bra and panties match. Black and silky. She couldn't look more sexy lying in just her underwear on the bed in front of me, and I need to have more of her. "God, you're sexy," I tell her before practically pouncing on her again to kiss her passionately.

I make my way back down her body and stop at her waist again. Her scent turns me on as I spread her legs, settling between them. I need to taste her. I drag her panties down, taking them off completely, and then I lick her pussy. She pulls on my hair and moans, her body beginning to writhe. I move my hands under her ass, gripping each cheek, and pull her closer to my mouth. She tastes amazing; I can't get enough of her. I give special attention to her clit, licking it softly, then sucking it into my mouth, then licking it again. It drives her crazy, and I just about lose all control when she says my name, but I don't let up. When I insert my finger, she loses it. Moving it in and out, Kelsey grinds her hips, and I know she's close. Before I know it, Kelsey's inner muscles clench down, and she comes, moaning my name once again.

Fuck, she's sexy. I need more of her! I crawl up and hover over her, looking into her eyes. She's still coming down from her orgasm, and I admire how beautiful she looks.

She swallows hard as if she's nervous, and then she tells me something I'm not expecting. "I've never had an orgasm that I didn't give myself. That was amazing."

I'm taken aback by her words. Did she really just say that I'm the first man to make her come? "You mean no one has ever made you come that hard before?" I ask for clarification.

She shakes her head, still coming down from her orgasmic bliss. "No. I mean you're the first man to ever make me come."

Her words hit me right in the heart, and I have to have her. I want to make her come again and again, make her feel other things she's never felt before. I want to do things to Kelsey that no man has ever done, and I want to make her mine.

Without saying another word, I quickly undress myself, then pull the condom I brought out of my pocket. I slide it onto my dick, then crawl back onto the bed. "I want you so bad, Kelsey. You turn me on like no other woman ever has." We kiss, and slowly, carefully I sink into her. "God, you feel so good," I say as I begin to move in and out of her. Her body feels incredible, and I can't help but moan in pleasure.

"Don't stop," she says. "You feel so good."

We kiss hard, and she rakes her fingernails down my back. Her legs wrap around my waist, and I sink a little deeper. I keep moving at a steady pace as we kiss, our hands exploring and stroking each other's bodies. I want to touch her everywhere and drive her even more wild, so I shift, rolling us over so she's on top. I take my hands in hers, linking our fingers together, and she begins riding me. In the soft light illuminating the room from the hallway, I can see in her eyes that she's in complete ecstasy, but she also seems a little nervous. "It's okay, baby. You're beautiful. Don't stop," I gently tell her. She holds my hands and looks down into my eyes. I can see the shift in her from a subtle unsureness to more confident, and I know she's all right.

I close my eyes for a moment, unable to keep eye contact with her any longer. There's just too much emotion, too much feeling, too much *loving* going on between us. I'm overwhelmed but in a good way. I'm in pure ecstasy.

I open my eyes again. My hands travel up her body and caress her breasts. When I pinch her nipples, she simultaneously grinds down on me, setting off another orgasm that rips through her. It takes me by surprise, and I ride it out. Before long, I'm coming, too.

A few minutes pass as we both catch our breaths. She's collapsed over me, and even though we're both a sweaty mess, we don't want to move away from one another. Eventually, Kelsey sits up so we're face to face, and she kisses me again. "That was …" Kelsey begins to say, but then stops.

"Amazing," I complete her sentence.

"Yeah, you could say that," she replies with a soft laugh.

"Are you okay?" I ask, remembering that she's never had a positive experience with sex. From the looks of it, though, this was definitely positive for her.

"I'm more than okay," she answers as she sits up. She gets off the bed and begins to pick her clothes up off the floor. I watch her, entranced with her beauty, and then she stops and looks at me. "Thank you, Brady."

With that, she disappears into the bathroom, closing the door behind her.

KELSEY

*H*oly. Shit. *That* is what everyone has been raving
about all these years! I finally experienced true, real
sex with a man who not only knew what he was doing, but also
cares for me more than any other man has before. I've never, *ever*
had sex like that before, let alone had an actual orgasm while
doing it! And not even just one but *two* orgasms!

I clean up and get dressed, but as I look at myself in the bathroom mirror, I wonder if I'm *over*dressed now. I decide to take
my pants off again, leaving me wearing just my underwear and
the plain white shirt I wore under my cardigan tonight. Then I
slip my bra off underneath my shirt, too. There. Now I look sexy.

At least, I think I do, anyway.

I brush my hair, which is a mess, and I realize I can't wipe the
smile off my face. Brady is such a nice guy, and I feel so lucky that
he has feelings for me, too. This is new territory for me, and I
don't want to mess it up. I know I'll have to keep my secrets
buried, but it'll be okay. I know I've turned my life around, and
what he doesn't know won't hurt him.

Opening the bathroom door, I walk back into my bedroom

and find Brady lying in my bed. He looks up at me and smiles. "Hey there."

I smile back at him. "Hey."

He puts his arm out as an invitation for me to lie next to him, so I do. It feels good to cuddle up next to him with his arm around me, holding me close. I place a hand on his bare chest as I rest my head on his shoulder. I notice he put his boxer briefs back on, but nothing else. I'm glad I took my pants, cardigan, and bra back off so I wasn't overdressed.

"How are you?" he asks, then kisses my forehead. His kind and gentle demeanor makes me relax and melt into him even more.

"I'm good," I reply, and I can't help but smile again. "Very good, actually."

"I'm glad to hear that," he says, stroking my hair. I close my eyes because it feels so good.

We lie like this together without saying anything for a while. This is something else I've never had before. Even with the few guys I slept with, we were done when we were done and didn't have any cuddle time afterward. But this is nice. My contentment lulls me to sleep until Brady's deep voice breaks the silence.

"Do you mind if I stay tonight?" he asks, and I realize that I hadn't even considered what would happen next. I want him to stay with me. I'm not ready for him to leave. I want to sleep through the night with him by my side.

"Yes, please stay," I reply, turning my head to look up at him so I can gauge his reaction.

He smiles at me. "I'm so glad you said that. I didn't want to leave." Then he kisses my forehead again, and I know that he really, truly likes me.

I relax back into his side and fall asleep.

. . .

When my alarm wakes me at 6 a.m., I'm momentarily startled to find Brady in bed with me. We drifted apart from each other during the night and didn't cuddle the whole night. Although it was nice to be so close to him, I'm sure it would've been uncomfortable to sleep like that all night. I think back to how wonderful last night was, and I smile at the memory.

I slide out of bed and go about my morning routine of getting ready for work. Brady is still sound asleep on his stomach with his head turned away from me, so all I see is the back of his head and his muscular upper back. Good lord, he sure is fit. His body is *nothing* to complain about.

After showering, I finish getting dressed and doing my makeup and hair in the bathroom. When I'm ready, I walk back into my bedroom, but Brady isn't there, and my bed is made. Did he leave already?

I hear a cupboard shut in my kitchen, so I know he's still here. I head down the hall into my living area and find him pouring coffee into two travel mugs.

"Good morning," he says with a smile on his face as I enter the kitchen.

"Good morning," I reply, surprised to find that he made coffee for me.

He sets the carafe back into the coffeemaker, then turns to me and wraps his arms around me. "You look beautiful," he says before planting a kiss on my lips.

I wrap my arms around him as we kiss. It goes on and on, and I don't want to pull away. I could spend all day just kissing Brady. I love his lips. And his tongue. And his hands touching me …

Jesus, what has he done to me? I've never had such strong feelings for a man, but I realize this isn't a bad thing. This is what I've always wanted but just never thought I deserved.

When Brady and I finally pull our lips apart, we don't let go of one another. We continue to hug, holding each other in a sweet embrace. "What time do you have to leave?" he asks.

"In about five minutes," I reply, still wrapped in him. I don't want to let go, and I wish I didn't have to go to work today.

"Can I cook you dinner tonight?"

I move my head back to look at him. "You want to cook for me?" This will be another first for me. A man has never cooked for me before.

He nods his head. "Yes. I actually enjoy cooking, so I'd love to have you over to my place tonight and make you dinner."

I smile, still in disbelief at how amazing Brady is. "I'd love that," I reply. "What time should I come over?"

"Is six o'clock okay?"

"Perfect."

We reluctantly let each other go, and I add creamer to the coffee he poured for me. He leaves when I leave for work but not before giving me one hell of a kiss. I drive to work with a perma-grin on my face that I hope doesn't fade away.

BRADY

*I*t's only been a month, but it feels like Kelsey and I have been dating much longer. Maybe it's because we knew each other first, and we weren't strangers who suddenly met. Whatever it is, I now know that time doesn't mean anything when you know the person is right for you. I'm sure Kelsey is the one for me. Tonight I'm finally going to tell her I'm in love with her, and I want us to see each other exclusively.

Not that either of us has dated anyone else in the past month, but I want to make it official. We've spent a lot of time together over the past five weeks. On the nights I don't work, and some nights when I actually get off on time, we spend the night together. Sometimes, it's at her place and sometimes at mine. We enjoy each other's company, and we get along really well. We spend our days texting each other, and on the nights when I work, I try to call her when I get the chance just to hear her voice. This is the type of relationship I've always wanted, and Kelsey is exactly the kind of woman I've wanted to be with. I feel like the luckiest man alive.

Of course, Nolan was elated when we told him we were dating. He said he couldn't think of anyone more perfect for either of us to be with, and I'd have to agree with him. Kelsey's parents were also excited to hear we were seeing each other, so I was glad to have her family's blessing. I've known the Richards family my whole life, so it would've been awkward if they didn't like the idea of me dating their daughter.

Kelsey hasn't met my parents yet, but that's the other thing I'm going to talk to her about tonight. Thanksgiving is next week, and although I have to work that day, my parents want to have Kelsey and me over for dinner the night before. I really hope she's willing to go with me and meet my family.

I'm cooking a roast for dinner, along with mashed potatoes, green beans, a salad, and rolls. I enjoy cooking dinner for Kelsey on my days off so she doesn't have to cook when she gets off work. I've always loved cooking, but it's hard to cook for just myself, so it works out really well. Plus, I get to spend more time with her.

When I hear the soft knock on my door, I quickly light the candles I set in the middle of the kitchen table, then hurry to let her in. "Hi, baby," I say when I open the door.

"Hi," she says before kissing me. I let her in, and she takes her coat off, hanging it on the coat hook by the door. "Dinner smells delicious. What are you making?"

"Beef roast and all the fixin's," I say as I wrap her in a hug. I can't get enough of this woman.

"Oh my gosh," she says, and I know she's noticed the kitchen table. I've never set the table for dinner like this before, but tonight is special, and I want her to remember it. She lets go of me and walks into the kitchen area. "What's all this?" she asks, motioning toward the table set with dishes and the lit candles.

I follow her, then place my hands on her hips and smirk. "We're having a fancy dinner tonight."

"What's the occasion?" she asks, bewilderment written all over her face. God, I love her. I wasn't planning to tell her like this, but I want to tell her how I feel.

"Kelsey," I begin, and suddenly, I'm nervous as hell. What if she doesn't love me back? I pause to just look into her eyes, trying to muster the courage I had just seconds ago.

"What is it?" she asks, and she rubs her hands up and down my arms. That does it. That simple touch from her puts me at ease, and I know once again the time is right.

"I want you to know something," I start again. I clear my throat because although I know the timing is right, I'm still nervous as hell. I take a deep breath and go for it. "Kelsey, I'm in love with you."

Kelsey freezes. Her hands stop on my arms, and she stares at me. "You … what?" she chokes out in a whisper.

Shit. I can't tell what she's thinking. Was this the wrong time? Am I screwing everything up between us?

"I love you," I say again, hoping I'd read her emotions right over the past few weeks. I thought she was falling in love with me, too.

Kelsey sucks in a breath, then covers her mouth with one of her hands. Her other hand is still firmly grasping my arm. Watching a tear form at the corner of her eye, I wipe it away, but then another forms. I wipe that one, too.

She moves her hand from her mouth and wipes her other eye. Jesus, I've made her cry. I still don't know if this is good or bad. "Brady," she starts, then stops to wipe her eye again. I use my hand to wipe her other one. She looks at me, and I brace myself for what she's about to say. "This past month with you has been amazing. I've never felt the way I do for you." She looks down, wiping her eyes again. I swear my heart has stopped beating. I'm on pins and needles waiting for her response. This moment will make or break our relationship. When she looks back up at me with a smile on her face but tears still on her cheeks, I still don't know what she'll say. "I love you, too," she says before grabbing my face in her hands and kissing me hard.

Thank God! I wrap my arms around her and kiss her with all

I've got. But kissing her isn't enough right now. Now that I've told Kelsey how I feel, I need to *show* her. I'm overflowing with emotions, and I just want to make love to her. "Fuck dinner," I say, and then go right back to kissing her. I start walking us toward my bedroom, not breaking our contact.

Kelsey

Brady drags me to his bedroom as we both claw at each other's clothing. By the time I'm lying on his bed, I'm down to my bra and underwear. Brady crawls over me in just his boxer briefs, then lowers his mouth to my neck, peppering kisses all the way down to my breasts. My body tingles with need, his kisses sending goose bumps all over my skin.

This past month has been incredible, and it's all because of Brady. He cares for me in a way I never thought I'd actually experience. Deep down, I always yearned to have a relationship like my parents or Nolan and Teresa's, but I truly never believed it would happen.

Brady unhooks my bra, pulling it off me, and his head drops to my bare breast. I arch my back as his tongue licks my nipple while his hand massages the other one. Everything this man does drives me wild, and I can't believe I ever pushed him away. I've done a lot of soul searching this past month, and I realized that what I always told myself was true; my past is my past, and I can't change that. All I can do is be the best person I can be now and look to the future. Brady didn't have anything to do with my past, and if I want to have any sort of future with him, I have to keep moving forward. Luckily, it helps that Brady's touch only makes me feel one thing now—complete ecstasy.

My body shivers as his hand and tongue skim their way down my body. When he reaches my underwear, he grips it in both hands and slides them down, then gently runs his hands back up my legs. His fingertips just barely graze my skin, feeling featherlight, and goose bumps form again. I suck in a breath as he spreads my legs and settles between them. Brady doesn't waste any time. My back bows off the bed as he glides his tongue against my clit, and I let out an uncontrollable moan. His skilled tongue licks it over and over, up and down, then side to side, driving me insane. When he adds a finger to the mix, pumping it in and out of me, I nearly combust. But I don't, not quite yet. He keeps up his ministrations, altering the pace and then inserting a second finger. My orgasm rips through me not long after, sending shockwave after shockwave through my body. I grip Brady's hair and practically scream in pleasure.

Before Brady, I had only ever experienced self-induced orgasms. I never knew how pleasurable sex could really be, and sex with Brady seems to exceed all my expectations. I truly never knew how good it could be, and now I can't get enough of Brady Danner.

Brady licks up every drop of my orgasm as I come down from the intense pleasure. Catching my breath, I place a hand over my chest. I look down at Brady and find him looking up at me. He smiles when we make eye contact, then he moves up and over me, not breaking our gaze.

"I love you," he rasps out before crashing his lips to mine. As he presses into my core, I tilt my hips up, feeling impatient to have him inside me. I love the way we fit so perfectly together, and the way his cock naturally curves up in just the right way to hit that spot deep inside me. It sets me off every time.

"I love you, too," I whisper as he slides into me. We both let out a moan, and my hands wrap around his neck. I want to be as close to him as I possibly can to show Brady how much he really means to me.

Brady moves at a slow but steady pace, kissing me all the while. If it's not my lips, his mouth and tongue are on my neck or my chest. The only time he stops is to say something sweet. *You're so amazing, you feel so good*, and *I fucking need you* are just a few of the sweet and sexy things he says as he fucks me. We've had a lot of sex since we started dating, but this time feels different for some reason. I feel closer to Brady than I ever have before. As if we've reached a new level in our relationship.

As I start to come apart at the seams, I can tell he is close, too. "Fuck, Kelsey," he growls as he quickens his pace.

I let out another moan as I feel the buildup, my body starting to teeter over that edge. "I'm gonna come," I say, breathlessly.

"Come with me," he says, breathless as well, still pounding into me at a delicious pace. And then it happens; my body explodes, coming hard, while Brady moans in pleasure, letting me know he's coming, too.

My arms grip onto him as we both fall apart. We've never come together before, and it's definitely a more intense feeling than when I just come alone. I feel a connection to him that I've never felt before, and I realize at that moment that I'm really, truly, head-over-heels in love with him.

Sure, I knew I loved him before. That's why I told him so when he confessed he was in love with me, too. But *this* feeling is different. If there's something stronger than love, that's what this would be. Is that even possible? Is there a stronger feeling than love? I don't know for sure, but what I do know now is that what I feel for Brady is both the scariest and most exciting I've ever felt, and I pray to God that what we have doesn't end.

BRADY

*a*fter making love to Kelsey, I feel a shift in our relationship—a good shift—as if we've reached a new level of intimacy. It's like nothing I've ever felt before, and it occurs to me that I love Kelsey in a way I've never experienced with another woman. She does something to me I can't explain. All I know is that I can't imagine my life without her now. She's the strongest woman I've ever met, especially after having turned her life around the way she did when she was younger. I admire her for the work she does at the high school, and she's one of the sweetest people I've ever met. Not to mention, she's beautiful, and the chemistry between us is explosive. I need Kelsey in my life.

We eat dinner in the candlelight, talking about our day. She tells me how that girl, Bridget, came to see her again today. Kelsey thinks she just needs someone to talk to, even if it's not about anything in particular. And she trusts Kelsey for some reason, which makes her feel like she might be able to make a difference in Bridget's life. I commend her for all she's doing to try to help this girl. Whatever her situation is, she obviously needs someone like Kelsey to help or just to listen.

After we finish eating, we continue to talk at the table, and I decide it's a good time to ask her about meeting my parents. "Kelsey," I start, hoping she's going be ready for this, "I have to work on Thanksgiving next week, so my parents invited me over for dinner the night before."

She nods in understanding, then takes a drink of her water. "That's nice. I'm sorry you have to work that day. It must be rough not to always have holidays off."

I smile at her comment. "Yeah, it's tough sometimes, but it's just a day. Celebrations can always take place, even if it has to be on a different date. I guess I've just always been used to it. My dad didn't always get holidays off either, so we'd sometimes have Christmas a couple of days early." I smile at the fond memory from my childhood. No matter what, Dad never missed celebrating a holiday, even if that meant that Santa came early, which I always thought made us kind of special.

Kelsey's face lights up as if she just remembered something. "I remember that about you!" She laughs, and I wonder what she means by that. "I had forgotten about it, but I remember Nolan complaining to my parents a couple of years because his friend got his Christmas presents early! It was like he couldn't understand what made you so special." She lets out another laugh and shakes her head. "I had forgotten all about that until now. Funny!"

I chuckle at the memory. "Yeah, my friends might have been a little envious. They just didn't understand ... and I *may* have bragged a little too much about it at the time."

Looking at Kelsey across the table from me, I momentarily get lost in her beauty.

"What?" she asks, suddenly looking at me skeptically.

Realizing I'm staring at her now, I shake my head, breaking eye contact with her. "Sorry," I say, then look back at her again. "You're just so beautiful."

She rolls her eyes and looks away, her cheeks blushing. Then she looks back at me and shrugs. "Whatever."

"You are," I tell her, knowing she won't accept this. Every time I tell her she's beautiful, she shrugs it off, and says, "Whatever." Even though she has trouble accepting a compliment, that doesn't stop me from always telling her.

Then I remember the question I have for her. "So, Kelsey, I didn't finish telling you about next week."

Kelsey cocks an eyebrow. "Okay …"

I take a deep breath, hoping she'll agree to meeting my parents. "Well, I've told my parents about us, and they want you to join us for dinner Wednesday night."

Kelsey's mouth drops open slightly, and both her eyebrows rise. She's surprised. And I can tell she doesn't know what to say because she's not saying anything.

"What do you think about that?" I ask, hoping for a good response.

She opens her mouth, as if she's going to speak, but then she doesn't. Shifting a bit in her chair, she sets her elbow on the table and rests her head against her hand. She squints at me, looking totally unsure of what to say. "Your parents want to meet me?"

I nod. "Yes, of course. They know we've been dating, and they want to have us over."

She clears her throat. "Um, does your dad remember arresting me?"

I nod again. "Yes, actually, he does. But he also understands that was close to twenty years ago, you've turned your life around, and you're now a high school counselor making a difference in the lives of teenagers."

"Okay …" she says, rubbing the back of her neck. She's unsure about this, but I need to convince her it's all right. My parents don't see her as the messed-up teenager she once was.

"Kelsey, it's really okay. You have nothing to worry about. My parents know I have strong feelings for you, and they want to get to know you better."

She takes a visible deep breath, sitting up straight in her chair and clasping her hands on the table in front of her. "I believe what you're telling me. I'm just worried that I'll be so nervous, I'll make a horrible impression."

"Baby," I say, reaching a hand across the table and placing it on hers. "There's nothing to worry about. I promise. Just be yourself. My parents are very down to earth. Dad has been retired for a few years, and he's so laid back now that he's not on the job. They're looking forward to meeting you, and"—I squeeze her hand to get her attention—"if we're going to be together, and I hope we are, you're going to have to eventually meet my parents."

Kelsey takes another deep breath. "I guess you're right." She looks away from me for a moment as she considers something. When she looks back at me again, her mouth curves up in a smile. "I hope we're going to be together, too. Okay, I'll go to dinner with you."

I let out a breath of relief. "Thank you, baby. I'm so glad you agreed. I can't wait for you to meet them."

KELSEY

*E*ver since I agreed to have dinner with Brady and his
parents, I've been a nervous wreck. I know he told me
not to worry, but that didn't calm my anxiety. His dad arrested
me. That memory is seared in my brain, and I'm sure his parents
have preconceived notions about me, regardless of what Brady
says.

It happened one night at a party. I had gone with my friends
to a house in Tenino, and of course, there was drinking and
drugs. I was high, but I'll never forget when the police showed up
and busted us all. I had a pipe in my hands when they caught us
plus a bag of weed in my pocket, so I was arrested. The chief of
police himself slapped the cuffs on me and took me to the
station. It's a small town, so even the chief was involved in the
noise complaint call a neighbor had phoned in about the party.

My parents both came to the police station to take me home,
but I now had an arrest on my record. I had to go to court, and
I was ordered to community service. I had to do hours of litter
cleanup at the city park as well as along the main road in town.
I felt like my parents were so ashamed of me, which only made
me go to a darker place than I already was. The truth was, I was

so ashamed of myself, I didn't think I could get help without bringing more shame to my family. I didn't think my parents would ever forgive me even though I now realize they were trying so hard to help me. I just kept turning them away as I continued to lie, rely on my "friends," and get deeper into drugs.

And now my boyfriend is the son of the man who arrested me. What are the chances of that? I guess, in a small town, those chances aren't that slim. However, it doesn't change how incredibly nervous I am to have dinner with them tonight. I've considered what to wear about a million times, and I've narrowed it down to three outfits, but I still can't decide among them. I have three hours until Brady picks me up, so I'm running out of time to calm my nerves.

I'm grateful I had the day off from school. We always get the day before Thanksgiving off so families can travel and get ready for the holiday. If I'd had to work today, it would have been hard to concentrate because I'm so on edge.

I make myself a cup of tea, hoping that will somehow help me to relax. I even watch an episode of my favorite show, but no such luck. T-minus two hours now, and I'm actually feeling more anxious than I was before. I decide to take a bubble bath to calm my nerves.

Just as I settle in the warm, lavender-scented bubbles, my phone rings. It's sitting on the edge of the tub, so I pick it up, excited to see it's my friend, Mari, calling.

"Hey, girl!" I answer.

"Kelsey! How are you? It's been way too long!"

"Yeah, it has! Besides seeing you on Facebook, it's good to hear your voice. Happy Thanksgiving!"

"You, too! Do you have plans with family tomorrow?"

I smile, just thinking about Brady. "Yes, I'm seeing my family tomorrow, but I'm actually having Thanksgiving today, too."

"Oh, really? Where?"

"My boyfriend's parents' house," I say, waiting to hear her reaction.

"Wait, what?" she asks in disbelief. For as long as I have known Mari, which has been since college, she has never known me to have a boyfriend. Sure, she knew the guys I dated over the years, but I've never had a serious relationship that involved meeting the guy's parents. "You have a boyfriend? Kelsey, you better start talking!"

I laugh. "It's hard to believe, right?"

"No ... well, yes," she says with a laugh. "Who is he? How long have you been with him?"

"His name is Brady," I start, and I tell her all the details of how we met, how he's friends with my brother, and how wonderful things have been with him so far.

"Wow," she says when I finish. "I have to say, you sound happier than I've ever heard you before. I'm happy for you."

"Thank you," I reply. Although Mari and I don't talk as often as I'd like, every time we do, we pick up right where we left off. Her opinion means a lot to me, so the fact that she thinks I sound happy makes me feel good.

"Maybe I'll have to come down to Yelm and visit soon. I'd like to meet Brady."

"You are welcome anytime! I'd love to have you visit," I tell her. Mari lives in Seattle, so it's over an hour drive away; sometimes closer to two hours with traffic.

"You're welcome to stay with me anytime, too," she offers. "It would be fun to have a night out in Seattle with you like the good old days."

"That would be fun," I reply. A night out in Seattle for us always involved eating dinner at a yummy restaurant, wandering around the busy downtown streets or Pike Place, and then picking up a delicious dessert to take home and devour as we sat in pajamas and watched a chick flick. Mari was never a partier, even in college, which made her the perfect friend for me.

We talk a little longer, catching up on our jobs and other things in our lives. Mari is a middle school counselor, so we always have interesting stories to share. Sometimes, we bounce ideas off each other for ideas on how to help kids. Of course, we did this a lot more when I still lived near her.

When we finally say goodbye and hang up, I feel refreshed. Talking to my friend felt good and calmed my nerves. I lie back in the tub and close my eyes, hoping this feeling stays with me.

Unfortunately, it doesn't. The second I remember that I'm meeting Brady's parents today, my anxiety sets in again. And now that I'm all cleaned up, it's time for me to get dressed. Wrapped in my bath towel, I stand in front of my bed with all three potential outfits laid out in front of me. I can't decide. What if I choose something too conservative? Or not conservative enough? Or something that just gives them a bad impression of the adult me? I don't know what to do.

And then my phone rings.

I pick it up off my bedside table and see it's Brady calling. I automatically smile and answer the phone. "Hi!" I try not to sound as nervous as I feel.

"Hey, baby. How are you doing?"

Should I tell him the truth? That I'm a bundle of nerves and may make a fool of myself tonight? "I'm okay. Just getting dressed," I say, keeping my tone light.

"I can't wait to see you," he says, his voice low and sexy.

I smile. Just hearing his voice and thinking about seeing Brady helps calm my nerves a bit. "I can't wait, either."

"Are you still nervous?" he asks. "Because you know you really don't need to be."

I roll my eyes. I know he means well, but he really has no idea how nerve-wracking this

is going to be for me. "I am, yes. I'm trying not to be, though. I'll be okay."

"I understand. If I didn't already know your family so well, I'd be nervous about meeting them, too."

Chuckling, I realize it's perfectly normal to be nervous when meeting your significant other's parents, but this isn't normal circumstances. Brady really has no idea how anxious I am about this evening.

"What's so funny?" he asks. "What are you chuckling about?"

"Oh, honey, I know you'd be nervous. But my dad never arrested you! I can't even decide on an outfit to wear."

"Baby," Brady says, and his tone lets me know he's being completely sincere in what he's about to say. "It's really going to be okay. Whatever you want to wear will be just fine because you always look nice. But if you want my opinion, I really like that blue, flowery blouse you wear with jeans and those brown boots. You just look like the perfect mixture of wholesome and sexy. Is that an option for tonight?"

I look at that exact outfit he just described laid out on my bed, and I smile. "Yes, it is, actually. Thank you for your opinion. I think I know what I'm wearing now."

"Great, baby. I'll let you finish getting ready, and I'll see you in about an hour, okay?"

I smile, so glad that I have such a kind and thoughtful boyfriend. "Okay, honey. See you then." We hang up, and I get dressed.

After I dress, I do my makeup and hair, all the while imagining how tonight will go. Brady keeps telling me it will all be fine, and I trust him, but I still have my doubts. I just don't want to make a fool of myself.

Right on time, Brady knocks, and I head to the front room to let him in.

"Hi," he says as he walks in and kisses me. "You look beautiful."

I roll my eyes. "Thanks. You look great, too."

"Stop rolling your eyes whenever I give you a compliment," he says playfully. "You are beautiful."

I roll my eyes again, this time on purpose, and then I smile at him. "I can't help it." I know I can't take a compliment without rolling my eyes. It's just the way I am.

Brady leans closer and kisses me again. "Well, try. Because I'm not going to stop complimenting you. Ever."

I smile at his words but feel my cheeks blush.

"Are you ready to go?" he asks.

"Yes. I guess so," I say with a chuckle. God only knows how tonight will go.

Brady drives us to his parents' house on the outskirts of town. My heart is pounding in my chest, and my palms are sweaty. I haven't had sweaty palms since middle school, and I keep wiping them on my pants, hoping they won't be clammy and gross when I meet his parents. Shaking someone's sweaty hand does not make a good impression!

When he pulls into the private driveway that I know leads to their house, I take a couple deep breaths. This is it. My future with Brady hinges on this evening. If his parents don't like me, there's no way he'll want to continue seeing me, and I refuse to come between him and his family. I take another deep breath—probably for the millionth time since we left my apartment—and wipe my hands on my legs once more just as Brady pulls up to their house.

My jaw drops.

Their house is huge.

I didn't expect this.

Brady must sense my surprise. "Are you okay?" He shuts the car off and places a hand on my knee.

I look at him, my eyes wide. "Your house is huge!"

Brady laughs and squeezes my knee. "Yeah, it's kind of big. But it's cozy on the inside. Don't let it intimidate you, okay?" He leans closer and kisses me, and I instantly relax a little. "Come on, let's go inside."

After we get out of his car, he takes my hand as we walk up the front steps. Seriously, who knew a police officer made enough money to live in a house like this? Although, now that I think about it, his dad was the *chief* of police for several years. I suppose the chief makes a lot more than a police officer patrolling the streets. The massive front porch spans the entire front of the house, wrapping around one side and probably continuing all the way to the back. The two-story house with large bay windows on both the first and second floors sits on a beautifully manicured piece of property, which is probably at least an acre.

We approach the grand entrance, and before we can even knock, the door flies open, and we're greeted by a very short gray-haired woman who's grinning from ear to ear. "Brady!" she exclaims as she wraps him in a hug.

"Hi, Mom," he says, hugging her in return. It's a reassuring sight to see him in such a sweet moment with his mom. He had told me he had a good relationship with his parents, but it's different to actually see them together.

When they pull away from their embrace, his mom immediately turns to me. "Kelsey!" she says with as much excitement as she greeted her son with, and before I know it, her arms are around me as well.

"Hi, Mrs. Danner," I say as I hug her in return. She's a few inches shorter than I am, probably making her four feet eleven. She's also thin, but from what I can tell now with my arms around her, she's a fit woman. I make a mental note to start working out more.

"It's so nice to finally meet you!" She pulls back from me, then takes both my hands in hers. "I remember your brother so well, and I can see the family resemblance, but you're much prettier!"

She winks, then drops one of my hands and turns, leading me into the massive house. "Come in!"

Brady and I follow her. Well, technically, she guides me since she's still holding my hand. I take in their home, and Brady described it perfectly when he said it was cozy. The staircase in the entryway leads to the second story, but his mom takes me into their living room, and I gaze out the floor-to-ceiling windows at their gorgeous property. To my right, I see an impressive kitchen with modern appliances and granite countertops.

"Have a seat," Mrs. Danner says as she lets go of my hand and sits on one of the sofas. I sit next to her, and Brady sits on the sofa across from us. "And, please, call me Betsy."

I smile at her. She's so kind, and now that I look at her again, I see that Brady takes after his mom. Many of their facial features are the same, and it's obvious that Brady is her son.

"Is Dad home?" Brady asks.

"Oh, yes," Betsy replies. "He was mowing the lawn earlier, so he took a shower to clean up. He should be downstairs in a few minutes."

"Your property is beautiful," I tell her. "How many acres do you have?"

She smiles kindly at me again. "Thank you! We love it here. We have two acres, which is a lot to take care of, but we wouldn't trade it for anything. Jim enjoys yard work, and riding the lawn mower is almost soothing for him."

Just then, a familiar man walks into the living room. I immediately recognize Chief Danner, the man who arrested me. Funny, but I can also see a resemblance between Brady and him. Brady's the perfect mix of both his parents.

My heart rate suddenly spikes. I'm nervous again, hoping his dad doesn't think of me as the stupid teenager I once was.

"Hello, young lady," he says, walking straight to me and

offering his hand, and I shake it. "I don't know if you remember me or not, but I'm Brady's dad. You can call me Jim."

"It's nice to see you again," I reply, and he places his other hand over mine. The kind gesture actually calms me a bit. Looking at him, he smiles at me, then squeezes my hand before letting go. He sits next to Brady on the other couch.

"So tell us about yourself," Betsy says. "Brady told us you're the new counselor at Yelm High."

"I am," I start, turning toward her and trying to make myself more comfortable. What a nerve-wracking experience this is, meeting his parents. I have *never* met a boyfriend's parents before, so I really have no idea what to expect. "I just started working there this school year, and I'm really enjoying my job so far. Before moving back here, I worked at Garfield High School in Seattle. I was tired of living in the big city, though, so as soon as the counselor position at Yelm opened, I applied right away. I'm so happy to be living back in my hometown."

"Brady can relate to that," his dad pipes in. "He wanted out of Portland so bad, he was ecstatic when Tenino Police had an opening."

"I have so much respect for school employees," Betsy says. "Working with our youth is such an important job. I'm sure it's not an easy one, either."

I chuckle. *That's* an understatement; nothing about my job is easy. "Thank you. It's stressful, but I also love it. I love helping teenagers who are struggling."

"That's very honorable," Jim says. "I'm glad to see you're doing so well in life."

I blush at his comment and smile. His parents don't seem bothered by my past, and I'm grateful. I relax a little more into the comfy couch, and we continue to chat. They share funny stories about Brady and his brothers when they were young, and I learn more about the man I'm in love with.

"Man, I wish Gary and Mike lived closer," Brady says, speaking of his brothers. He'd told me about them before, and although life has taken them in different directions, Brady is still close with both of them. Gary, the eldest, is five years older than Brady, and he lives in southern California with his wife and kids. Mike is the middle brother, just two years older than Brady, and he lives in Las Vegas, also married with kids. While Gary did not follow in their father's footsteps to work in law enforcement, Mike did, and he's the head of a large casino group's security department.

Betsy and Jim ask about my family, fondly remembering Nolan as a good friend of Brady's. They remember my parents as well, so I fill them in on what they're doing now; still working but both close to retirement.

Suddenly, a timer goes off in the kitchen, and Betsy jumps up, heading toward the kitchen. "Oh, that would be the turkey."

"I didn't realize you were cooking a turkey tonight," Brady calls to her.

"Your mom insisted on cooking a full Thanksgiving dinner tonight," Jim explains as Betsy works in the kitchen. "She said there's no point in making a big fuss about it tomorrow when it's just the two of us here, and I agreed."

"Wow, thanks, Mom," Brady says.

"You're welcome," Betsy replies, placing a large pan on the counter. I can see a turkey sticking out the top, and the smell is divine.

"Do you need help, dear?" Jim asks his wife.

"You could set the table and pour the wine," she says.

"I'll help, too," Brady says as he and his dad both stand, so I decide to be helpful, too. All three of us go to the kitchen, and Brady and his dad start pulling things from the cupboards to place on the dining room table. I help by taking the dishes that Brady hands me.

After we finish setting the table, we help Betsy carry the food to the dining room as well. It's nice to see their family helps one another, and I feel as if they're accepting me. When Jim asks if I'd like red or white wine, and I politely decline, he eyes me for a moment, then smiles. "Do you not like wine?"

I feel my cheeks blush once again. "No, I just don't drink alcohol."

Realization crosses his features, and his eyes soften. "Well, that's wonderful, Kelsey. I'm impressed by you."

Brady politely declines wine to drink as well, and I give him a look as if to say, *you can have some; don't worry about me.* But he ignores me, still refusing to drink, and pours ice water into both of our wine goblets. Kissing me on the cheek, he whispers in my ear, "I love you."

I smile at him, and then he turns and walks back into the dining room, carrying both our glasses.

Dinner is delicious, and we have a nice time with his parents. We get to know each other better, and all the nerves I felt earlier wither away. Brady's parents don't seem bothered by the fact that I was once a troubled teenager who Jim had arrested. All they care about is who I am now, and they seem impressed with how I turned my life around.

After dinner, we all help clear the table while Betsy starts washing the dishes. Just as I bring the last dish to the kitchen and place it on the counter with all the others, Jim looks at me, obviously noticing something.

"Do you have a scar above your eye?" he asks, and I'm taken aback. My scar is so faint now, I forget it's there most of the time. Brady has never even mentioned it to me before; in fact, no one has asked me about my scar in ages.

I touch my forehead above my left eye, feeling my skin. I do still feel a slight indentation where my scar remains. "Just a little one now," I reply, still surprised he noticed it.

Betsy turns off the faucet and looks at me. "What scar?" she asks.

Brady, who had been in the bathroom, walks into the room at

that moment. "What are you guys looking at?" he asks, wondering why his parents are both examining my forehead.

Jim answers. "Oh, just Kelsey's scar." He turns to Brady, then steps away from me, placing some food in the fridge.

Betsy is still looking closely at my forehead, then drops her gaze to my eyes and smiles, apologetically. "I can barely see it," she reassures. She returns to washing dishes at the sink.

"What scar?" Brady asks, sounding confused.

"I told you," Betsy says, "it's hardly noticeable. I don't know how your dad even saw it."

"Well, I was there when she got it," Jim announces as he closes the refrigerator door.

Shame washes over me, and I look at the ground, wringing my hands together tightly. *Shit!*

"Wait, what?" Brady asks, still utterly confused. He moves closer to me and places a hand on my chin, slowly moving my head up so he can look at me. "Where is it?" he asks, his voice gentle and soothing. It helps me relax a little again.

"It's above my left eye," I tell him as I point at it, my voice soft.

Brady looks carefully, then makes eye contact with me again. "How'd it happen?" he asks before placing a kiss on both my cheeks.

I take a deep breath, then reply, "I was in a bad car accident."

Brady doesn't say anything. He just kisses me again, this time on my forehead, then takes my hand. "Let's go talk in the living room."

BRADY

a car accident? After all the conversations Kelsey and I have had, why has this never come up? I never even noticed her scar before, but now that I see it, I can't *unsee* it. I'm more than a little curious to find out what happened to her.

Dad, Kelsey, and I all sit in the living room while Mom finishes loading the dishwasher. Dad has an apologetic look on his face.

"I'm sorry, Kelsey," he says, and I can tell he's being sincere. "I didn't know that Brady didn't know about it. I just remember that night very well. You're very lucky to be alive."

I look at Kelsey, sitting next to me, and she nods. "It's okay," she says to Dad. "I *am* lucky to be alive … I just don't like to talk about that night. There's no way you could have known that, though, so don't worry about it."

"What happened?" I ask, hoping she'll talk about it now. I feel bad that this is something she doesn't like to recall, but considering my dad was *there,* I'd like to know what happened to her.

Kelsey looks down, wringing her hands together in her lap. That's a telltale sign she's nervous. I gently place my hand over hers, and she looks up at me. I give her a small smile, hoping she understands that I love her and want to know everything about her, even the sad stuff.

Her lips curl a fraction into a sad smile. "Well, I had been at a party with some friends all the way out in Bucoda," she starts to explain, and I give her my full attention. "We were high, which was nothing unusual. This guy I was friends with, Josh, was the driver that night, and he was going fast. He didn't make a curve in the road, and he ran off the road, crashing head-on into a tree." Kelsey looks down again. "Josh and the guy sitting in the front seat—I didn't know his name—both died. The three of us in the back seat were seriously injured and wound up in the hospital."

Holy shit. This wasn't just a *bad* car accident; this was traumatic! No wonder she doesn't like to talk about it!

Dad speaks up, his voice soft. "I arrived on the scene and recognized Kelsey. She was unconscious and in pretty bad shape. She was really lucky that night." He clears his throat, and I look at him. He looks as though he might cry, and I think it's because he realizes how stupid it was of him to bring this up in the first place. I know he didn't mean to upset Kelsey. "I'm sorry I brought it up," he apologizes, looking at Kelsey sincerely.

Kelsey looks up at him with a small smile on her face. "It's okay. Thank you for saving me that night," she says. "I'm thankful I got a second chance to do things right in my life."

"Of course," Dad replies. "And you've done things better than just right. You've come full circle now to help kids who may be making bad choices in life. You're doing great things, Kelsey. I'm proud of you."

"Thank you," Kelsey says, her voice cracking. I see tears forming in her eyes, and I automatically wipe them for her. *Fuck!* We were having such a nice evening, and now this. I know Dad didn't mean for it to happen. I rack my brain, trying to think of how we can recover from this.

Then Mom comes into the room and sits next to Dad. "I have some news," she says, changing the subject. We all look at her, wondering what she's going to announce. "I just got a text from your brother, Gary. He's going to come up for Christmas! Isn't that great?"

"That's awesome!" I haven't seen Gary and his family in over a year, so it will be good to see them. "How long are they staying?"

"He said they'd be here for a few days. I'm not sure if they've bought their airfare, so they might not know yet. I told them they could stay here."

"It'll be great to see them," Dad says.

We spend another hour or so at Mom and Dad's. We have a nice time talking about all sorts of things … but nothing more about Kelsey's past. She relaxes a lot more, too, and I can tell my parents really like her. When we say goodbye to them, Mom gives her a hug and tells her she's welcome here anytime. Dad hugs her as well, saying he hopes to see her again soon. What a relief it is to know that my parents like the woman I've fallen in love with. I can't wait to see Gary next month, and not just because it's been so long; I want him to meet Kelsey, too.

As I drive home, Kelsey takes my hand in hers and rests it on her thigh. "I really like your parents," she says.

"Good," I reply. "They liked you, too."

"Did they?" she asks, sounding unsure. Her thumb rubs against my hand in a nervous fashion.

"Yes, of course," I reassure her. "Why wouldn't they?"

"I don't know," she replies. She looks out the window and doesn't say anything else for a moment, but then she speaks again. "I'm sorry I never told you about the accident before tonight. That was kind of awkward."

I give her hand a slight squeeze. I don't want her to feel bad about this; it was obviously a difficult thing for her to talk about tonight. "Don't worry about that, baby. It happened a long time ago, and I'm just glad you're here with me now." Then a thought occurs to me. "Was this the thing about your past that you've been afraid to talk about?"

When Kelsey looks at me and doesn't say a word, I wish I could read her mind. I'm dying to know what happened to her as a teenager that she doesn't want to talk about. This accident obviously had a huge effect on her life, but if this isn't *the* thing she's still hiding from me, I don't know what it could be.

She shakes her head, then looks out her window again. "No … although this was pretty horrific. I almost died, and I wish I could forget everything about that night. It's what led to me being kicked out of school."

I whip my head to look at her briefly, then turn my attention back to the road. "It was? How?" I ask, curious to know what happened.

"Well, after they determined all five of us in the car were high and in possession of drugs, the high school decided to search our lockers. They found a small bag of heroin in mine, and with the zero-tolerance policy, I was expelled. I was still in the hospital, but it didn't matter; they kicked me out immediately."

Shit. I had no idea. And this *isn't* the worst thing that's happened to her?

"Of course, now I totally agree with how the school handled it," she continues. "And though the accident almost took my life, it's what ultimately saved it. It was a huge wake-up call for me when I had to switch schools and I was forced to get clean."

I rub her hand with my thumb. I'm more than curious now about what she still doesn't want to tell me. If almost dying and being expelled from school for possession of heroin isn't the worst thing that happened to her, then what the hell is it? I can't force her to tell me, though. I need to work up to her feeling comfortable enough to talk about it.

"Baby, I'm so glad you survived that crash, and that it helped you get sober. I can't imagine not having you in my life now." I lift her hand to my mouth to kiss.

"Thanks," she says, and out of the corner of my eye, I see her wipe hers.

"Honey, don't cry," I say as I kiss her hand again.

"I'm okay," she says with a hitch in her voice as she continues to wipe her eyes. My stomach drops; I hate seeing her sad. I wish I could make it all better for her so she doesn't have such terrible memories.

"You know I love you, right? Your past doesn't change how I feel about you. You're an amazing woman now, and I feel lucky to have you in my life." I kiss her hand again, hoping she knows how serious I am, and how much I really do love her.

She sniffles and wipes her eyes once more. "I know. I love you, too, and I feel so lucky to have you in my life. You're so understanding … I couldn't ask for a better boyfriend."

My heart swells with joy, knowing she feels the same as me. I've never been in a relationship like this before. My past girl-friends have always been too needy, and they couldn't handle my profession. If I suddenly had to work overtime and break a date, they often got upset and didn't understand I had no choice in the matter. One girlfriend even begged me to switch careers because being a police officer was too dangerous. Kelsey is different, though. She has never gotten upset if I had to work overtime, nor has she complained about my job at all. In fact, she genuinely seems interested whenever I tell her what happened on my shift. Likewise, I'm genuinely interested in her job, and I think she's amazing at what she does.

"So," Kelsey says, her voice sounding a bit more upbeat, "am I staying at your place, or are you staying at mine tonight?"

I look at her and smile as I come to a stop at a traffic light. "Your choice. It doesn't matter to me."

"Okay, then you can come to mine," she says, then winks at me.

I drive the rest of the way home, which isn't that far. After dropping Kelsey off at her apartment, I go to mine to grab a change of clothes for tomorrow. I already have a toothbrush and razor at Kelsey's apartment, and she keeps a few things at my place as well. If things keep going as well as they are now, I can see us eventually moving in together. However, as much as I love her, I want her to be completely honest with me before making that big of a commitment. I don't want to have any secrets between us if we're living together.

God, I hope she tells me her secret soon.

KELSEY

*A*fter Brady drops me off at my apartment, I do a quick cleanup. Brady has actually spent the past few nights here with me. I'd come home from work, and then he'd come over. Sometimes, it's the other way around, and I stay at his place, but this week, we've been at mine. I love spending time with him, and we're becoming more and more comfortable with each other.

Meeting his parents today went a million times better than I expected it to. Although there was the hiccup when the topic of my accident came up, it still went well. His parents seem to like me, and now Brady knows another piece of my past. Really, the only thing he still doesn't know about is the worst thing I have to tell him. I want to tell him—I really do—but I don't know how it will affect his feelings for me. I love him so much, and I really can't imagine what I'd do without him in my life now.

Just as I finish loading the dishwasher, I hear a knock on my door. I walk to the entryway and let Brady in. He greets me with a kiss as he always does. I close my eyes and allow myself to melt into him. Brady shuts the door with his foot, and his kiss deepens. Before I know it, my back hits the wall, and his body is flush against mine. I let out a moan as he presses his hips into mine. I feel his hard-on push against my core, and it turns me on even more. I'm always turned on when Brady's around, which I'm still getting used to. Sex used to mean nothing to me; I never wanted to have it, and I was fine living a celibate life. But it's different with Brady. It's always a good experience, and I can't seem to get enough of it with him.

"I want you," he says as he moves his hand under my shirt, skimming his fingers across my skin.

"I want you too," I whisper between kisses. We continue to kiss, and I feel myself getting more and more desperate for him. Forget going to my room; I start walking him toward the couch. He sits, and I climb onto his lap, rubbing my core against his bulge. He moans into my mouth, so I do it again, and he grips my ass as tight as he can.

"You're so sexy," he says, pulling his lips away from mine only long enough to say it.

I move my hands down to pull his shirt off. He helps me, then he undresses me as well. I reach around and undo my bra, letting it fall to the ground. He stops and looks at me with pure adoration, topless, straddling him on his lap.

"You're all mine," he says, his voice a whisper, but I know he means it with conviction.

"Yes, I am," I say, then I move closer to him, kissing him again, madly and deeply. I'm claiming him with this kiss. He's all I want; all I've *ever* wanted.

"Get up," Brady says suddenly. I look at him, wondering why he would want me to get up now, but I stand and ask him what's wrong. "Nothing," he replies with a sexy smirk on his face, and he stands as well. "Sit down."

When I sit back down on the couch, Brady kneels in front of me, spreading my thighs apart so he can fit between them. His hands snake around my waist, and his mouth finally finds mine again. Before I know it, he's pulling my pants down, and I lift slightly so he can take them off. He takes my underwear along with them, so I'm left naked sitting in front of him.

Brady rubs his hands up and down my thighs, then he spreads my legs apart again, leaving me totally exposed to him. He looks at me. I should feel self-conscious, but the look on his face just makes me feel wanton. His gaze slowly moves up my body until we make eye contact. "You're so fucking sexy." Wrapping his arms around my thighs, he pulls my body closer to the edge of the couch and lowers his head to start licking my pussy.

His tongue slides up and down my folds, stopping to tease my clit every so often. It feels so good, so amazing, and I writhe on the couch and moan in pleasure. When he inserts a finger and slides it in and out while simultaneously sucking my clit into his mouth, it's my undoing. I call out his name and come harder than I have in a long time. Every time Brady and I are together, it's amazing, but he really does know how to use his tongue for my benefit.

I try to get my breathing under control and relax from my orgasm. Before I know it, Brady shifts me to lie down on the couch. Then he gets on top of me, settling between my legs. He gently brushes his fingers through my hair. I look at him and smile.

"You feel so good," I say, but my voice is barely louder than a whisper. My body is still vibrating, singing with pleasure.

He smiles at me, still stroking my hair. "I love making you come. I want to do it again."

I feel his cock against my sex, and then he slides into me, slowly. Sensuously. Lovingly. Once he's fully seated, he doesn't move. He looks in my eyes and runs his fingers through my hair once more. "I love this. Being close to you, feeling your body beneath mine."

I reach up and run my hand down his cheek, then around to the back of his neck. I pull him down to meet my lips. I kiss him hard, and he starts moving. I love this, too. The way his body envelops me as if he's protecting me. His strokes are rhythmic, but he breaks the rhythm at times so I feel a different sensation. I love him. I love what he does to my body. I never thought I'd have these kinds of feelings, and now I don't think I'll ever get enough of him.

It doesn't take me long to come again since his oral skills have already left me sensitized. "Oh, God, Brady," I call out as my body shakes with pleasure. He doesn't stop, though. He keeps pounding into me at a delicious pace, and I know he's close when he rests his forehead against mine.

I've barely recovered from my last orgasm when he whispers, "You feel so fucking good. Come with me." And I do. I moan loudly, unable to control myself. It's so intense, and Brady captures my mouth with his, kissing me like his life depends on it.

We lie together, trying to catch our breaths, not saying a word, but every once in a while, we kiss. Brady is always so gentle with me, and I know I'm a lucky woman. When we finally do get up, we pick up our clothes and head to clean up. Instead of putting on the same clothes, I put on my pajamas. Brady meets me in my room after using the bathroom in the hall.

"It's getting late. Do you want to get in bed?" he asks.

I look at the clock and am surprised to see it's already almost ten o'clock. At least I don't have to work tomorrow. The only plan I have is to be at my parents' house for Thanksgiving around noon. I wish Brady didn't have to work so he could go with me.

"Yeah, we probably should. It's getting late, and you have to work tomorrow," I reply as I start to pull the covers back on the bed.

Brady walks to the other side of the bed to pull the covers down as well. "So, I was thinking," he starts, and I stop and look at him. "We stay together most nights of the week now … and I really enjoy all the time I get to spend with you, Kelsey." He stops messing with the covers and looks at me as well. "Have you ever thought about what it would be like if we just lived together?"

My heart skips a beat. Did he really just ask me that? I'm not sure if I should jump up and down with joy—because I *have* thought about how nice it might be to live with Brady—or if I should panic. We haven't been together *that* long ... Isn't it too soon to be thinking about moving in together?

I clear my throat and look away from Brady. When I dart my gaze back to him, he looks nervous. Shit! Have I already messed this moment up before even saying a word? God, I hope not. I need to speak.

"Brady, I have thought about living with you. I really have." His face falls even more, and he looks crestfallen and defeated. *Fuck!* I need to salvage this conversation without hurting him any further. "I want to live with you, honey. I do. I'm just worried we're moving too fast."

Brady cocks an eyebrow, and his lips move up a fraction. "Baby, I know it's kind of soon, but I feel like what we have is right. Doesn't it feel right to you?"

I nod my head. "Yes, of course, I do. But we've only been together for about a month! Not only that, we're both locked into our leases for about six more months."

He walks back around to my side of the bed, stopping just in front of me. "I know. And you're right; we should wait a little longer. I guess waiting at least until our leases are up is a good thing." He chuckles, then kisses me sweetly on the lips. Thank goodness he agrees with me. As much as I love Brady and can actually see a future with him, I think we'd be nuts to move in together so soon.

"I'm glad you agree with me. I think we need to continue to get to know each other first," I say. Brady squints at me as if he's trying to figure something out. "What is it?" I ask, wondering what he's thinking.

He shakes his head, then says, "I guess I'm just really curious to know everything about you. Even the bad stuff." Brady takes both my hands in his and takes another step closer to me. He kisses my forehead, then says, "Tell me what you're so afraid to say. What's your big secret from your past that I still don't know?"

I look up at him, and my heart pounds. He really wants to know my secret, but I don't know if I can tell him. "Brady, it's …" I'm suddenly so nervous, and I don't even know what to say. I pull away from him and walk across the room.

"Kelsey, I feel like you're hiding this horrible thing that happened to you, and that maybe it's not quite as horrific as you think it is. Please, I just want to know what happened."

I look at him, wringing my hands together. I can't tell him. Not yet. Maybe never. And I hope he understands I have to keep this to myself. "But it really is as bad as I think it is, and you'll probably look at me differently when I tell you."

"I love you, Kelsey. Nothing is going to change that."

"This probably will," I reply, then turn away from him. *Fuck!* We were having such a nice evening together, and now this! My past really is going to haunt me for the rest of my life.

Brady approaches me, placing his hands on my arms. "Please, Kelsey. You'll feel better to get it off your chest."

I turn around to face him again, and I feel the tears welling up in my eyes. "I can't."

Brady's eyebrows knit together. "You can't? Or you won't?"

"It's complicated." I move out of his grasp and sit on the edge of my bed.

"Will you ever be able to tell me?" he asks, and the question hangs in the air. I actually don't know the answer to it. I look at Brady, unable to say anything, simply because I don't know what to say. "I guess that's a no," he says, sounding defeated, sad, and disappointed.

"I'm sorry," I say, my voice cracking. "I want to tell you, I really do, but it's just too much."

"Kelsey," he says, his voice louder and more upset than before. I've really ruined tonight. "What the hell is so terrible that you can't even tell me? It happened nearly twenty years ago! I know you're not the same person you were then, so I'm not going to judge you or fall out of love with you. However, if you have to keep this secret, I may not be able to trust you like I thought I could."

His words slice right through my heart. I know I'm hurting him, and it's killing me. If only I could just tell him what happened, but it's not that easy. Then a thought occurs to me: he's hiding something from me, too.

"Brady, why did you leave Portland?" I ask, looking him square in the eye.

He scrunches his face, obviously confused by my sudden question. "What are you talking about? What does that have to do with this?" he asks.

I stand, crossing my arms in front of me. He never wants to talk about this and always gives a canned response. He's obviously hiding something as well. "You never want to talk about why you left Portland and moved back here. Way back at Nolan's Fourth of July party, I noticed the slight reaction you had when you were asked the question, and then you gave a very short answer. So, tell me, what's the real reason?"

Brady crosses his arms as well, and I can tell I've hit a nerve with him. Well, good, because he hit a nerve with me. "Kelsey, I just wanted a change and to move back home. That's it."

"Then why are you so defensive?" I ask.

Brady scoffs and throws his arms up. "I don't know what you're talking about!"

"I think you do. I'm not the only one with a deep, dark secret, am I?"

Brady glares at me. I've never seen him so mad. I've really pissed him off, and now I'm worried what will happen next. I don't want Brady to leave. I love him, and I want him in my life. I really didn't mean to make him so angry, but it was the only way to get the subject away from my own secret. And I truly do believe he's hiding something.

"Kelsey, drop it." Ahh, there it is. Proof he does have a secret. If he didn't, he wouldn't tell me to drop it.

"What? You don't like it when the table's turned on you?" I ask, and I realize I'm really pissed off now, too. How dare he question me about my past when he's not willing to tell me about his!

Brady's face turns a darker shade of red, and it makes my blood boil even more. "I think I'll go home now," he says, then strides out of the room.

I follow him to the living room. He stops and picks his shoes up to put on. Is he really going to leave? Sure, I'm mad at him right now, but I'd rather he stay so we can work through this.

However, that probably means I'd have to end up telling him my secret, and I definitely can't do that now. Fuck. Maybe he should go home so we can both cool off.

"I'll call you tomorrow," he mumbles as he ties his shoes. When he's done, he looks at me, and says, "I love you, Kelsey, and I want to live with you someday. But I can't be in a relationship with someone who keeps a secret."

I look him square in the eye, and reply, "Neither can I."

We stare each other down for a moment before he turns and opens the door. "Have a good night," he says as he leaves, closing the door behind him.

I'm frozen in place, unable to move or think for a moment. What the fuck just happened? Brady and I had an amazing day together, he came over to spend the night, we had incredible sex, and now this! How quickly things can change from great to shitty. What the hell am I going to do?

BRADY

Fucking hell. After the argument Kelsey and I had last night, I didn't think today could get any worse. My shift isn't even half over, and I've already had two domestic disturbance calls that resulted in trips to jail and lots of paperwork. You'd think Thanksgiving would be a slow day at work, but the truth is, when families get together, the disagreements can often lead to fights. Who knew a small town like Tenino would have so many?

I still haven't called Kelsey even though I said I would. I haven't texted her, either. We haven't talked in any way since I left her apartment last night, and it's killing me. I love her, but if she's not willing to be totally honest with me, I don't see how our relationship can progress.

However, she also somehow knows I'm not being completely truthful with her. I didn't just move back here to be close to my family. I loved working in Portland … until reality hit me. It's hard enough to think about that night, let alone talk about it. I didn't think I would ever have to talk about it again, but somehow, Kelsey knows I'm hiding something.

Just as I'm finishing the last of my paperwork for my second arrest, I feel my personal phone buzz in my pocket. For some reason, I have a feeling it's Kelsey, and when I check my phone, my suspicion is confirmed.

Kelsey: *Hi. I haven't heard from you yet today. I just wanted you to know I'm thinking of you.*

Shit. I love her so much. How can I be mad at her for having trauma in her life? I mean, it must be really bad if she can't just come out and tell me about it. Isn't that why I can't talk about the real reason I moved back?

I text her.

Me: *I hope you had a good day with your family. I'm thinking about you, too. Work has been busy today, so I haven't had a chance to call you yet. I will try to later. Love you.*

There. I slide my phone back into my pocket, then pick up the paperwork in front of me to go turn in. As soon as I'm done, my phone buzzes again.

Kelsey: *I love you, too.*

Thank God. I was worried that I hurt her too much last night, and she might've re-examined her feelings for me. I need to call her as soon as I get back in my car, where I'll have some privacy.

But as soon as I get in the driver's seat, another call comes in from dispatch. This time, it's for disorderly conduct at one of the local bars. I guess I'll have to wait and call Kelsey later.

A few hours later, I still haven't had a chance to call her. Thanksgiving is not a dull day around here, that's for sure. I always expected this in Portland, but I thought things would be quieter here. I guess I was wrong.

Finally, I get a quiet moment in my car. I'm starving, so I pull out my lunch to eat. Then I take out my phone. I have messages from both of my brothers. Kelsey hasn't contacted me again, though. Hopefully she's not mad at me. I can't help that I've been busy at work and not had the chance to call. I need to take advantage of this downtime and call her. I pull up her number and call. It rings once … twice … three times … four … and then it goes to her voicemail. Shit! Is she busy, or is she still too mad to talk to me? I hang up without leaving a message. She'll see that I called and hopefully call me back.

Suddenly, my phone rings. But it's not Kelsey's name on the screen. It's my buddy, Scott. I answer right away. "Long time, no see, brother!"

"Happy Thanksgiving, Danner. How're things in Timbuktu, or wherever it is you're working now?"

I laugh. "Tenino, shithead, but close enough. It's busy as fuck here today! Domestic call after domestic call. I guess it doesn't matter if you're in a big city or a small town; if you've got family drama, the holidays are going to be dramatic."

Scott chuckles. "Yeah, I guess so. How have you been, man?"

"I've been good. How are you?"

"Never better. And I got today off from work, so that was a bonus. Not only is it Thanksgiving, but it's also Jackson's first birthday! We've been celebrating all day, and I even got to have Ellie for a few days."

"Jesus, has it been a year already?" I ask, surprised that Scott's son is already a year old. It seems like yesterday he was born.

Ellie is his daughter, who lives with her mom in Seattle, but he gets visitation.

"Yeah, it's hard to believe. Time goes by so fast! Ellie's already two. I'm lucky Brooke is letting me take her for longer periods of time now. Since having Jackson, I can see how much I missed with Ellie when she was a baby."

Scott went through a rough time, which resulted in Brooke and him getting divorced shortly after Ellie was born. It was extremely hard on him, but he also happened to meet Lisa shortly after they separated. It was completely by chance, and it turns out they're perfect for each other. Timing is a bitch and made it seem as if he moved on really fast, but he was relieved when Brooke, too, moved on when she reconnected with her high school sweetheart. Long story short, things worked out better for them both, and I've never seen Scott more happy.

"How is Brooke, by the way?" I ask. I knew Brooke pretty well when they were married. She was always sweet to me and all the other officers in Portland. I felt bad for her when Scott fucked their marriage up, so I was relieved to find out she's doing really well now, too.

"Brooke is doing well. She and Ryan are actually expecting."

"Is that right? Good for them!"

"Yeah, I think she's due in May."

Suddenly, dispatch comes through again. Scott holds on while I listen to the call, which is for an auto accident out on the highway to Bucoda. Fuck. I *hate* traffic accidents, especially on holidays. Nothing's worse than having to notify a family that their loved one has passed, when it's supposed to be a nice day of family memories. It's dark out now, and many people have been consuming alcohol today, so I have a feeling this accident may be really bad.

"Sorry, man, I gotta go," I tell Scott as I put on my seat belt and get ready to go.

"No problem. I'll talk to you later. Stay safe out there."

"Thanks. And Happy Thanksgiving to you and the fam."

We hang up, and I drive with lights and sirens out to the location of the accident. It doesn't take me long to get there, and I'm relieved to find I'm not the first to arrive. A fire truck and ambulance are already on the scene, and another Tenino officer pulls up behind me. Unfortunately, just as I suspected, the accident is pretty bad. It looks as if one car crossed the double yellow lines, causing them to hit head-on. If both the drivers survived, I'll be shocked. The cars are in such a mangled mess, I can't even tell the make or model of either one of them. I pray there are no kids involved.

As I approach the scene, a firefighter stops me. "Hey. Both drivers are injured. We're getting the jaws of life to extract them. I wouldn't be surprised if this turns out to be a fatality."

"Fuck. I'll close the road." I head back to my car and grab the flares to block the road. The other officer, whose name is Mitchell, helps me, and we quickly have the road shut down to traffic. People will be pissed about having to turn around, but with this accident possibly being a fatality, we'll thoroughly investigate, which means we can't have any cars driving through.

"Jesus," Mitchell says as he walks back from watching the firefighters use the jaws of life. "Those are high school kids in the car."

My heart drops, and I rub my forehead. Notifying family members that a loved

one was seriously injured—or killed—in an accident is hard enough when it's an adult. Teenagers? That's one of my worst nightmares.

Before we know it, several more officers have arrived as well as additional firefighters and ambulances. As we watch them load the accident victims onto the gurneys, a thought occurs to me. "Mitchell, how do you know they're in high school?"

"There's a Yelm High parking pass in the window, and they looked young, from what I could tell."

Shit! "Did you say Yelm?"

"Yeah. Why?"

"Fuck. My girlfriend is a counselor at that school. She probably knows these kids."

I walk toward the mangled cars to get a better look. I find a firefighter who's standing to the side. "Hey, are these teenagers?"

He looks at me with a solemn look on his face. "Yeah. It's a miracle they're all still alive. Even the driver and passenger in the other car are still breathing."

Well, that's a relief. At least it's not a fatality ... yet anyway.

I hang around, waiting to find out the teenagers' names. When I finally find out, I call Kelsey. There's really nothing for me to do on the scene except make sure traffic doesn't drive through.

Kelsey picks up on the third ring. "Hey," she says.

"Hey, honey. Sorry I haven't been able to call. I'm still at work, and I'm actually at the scene of an accident right now."

She's silent for a moment before saying a long-drawn-out, "Okay ..."

"I don't want to freak you out, but I thought you should know that one of the cars involved was full of teenagers from Yelm High."

She gasps. "Oh, no! Are they okay?"

"For now, they are. I got their names, if you want to know."

"Oh my God, yes. Tell me who was involved," she says, her voice laced with panic. It kills me that she's so upset by this, but of course she is. She loves her job and the kids she works with.

I look at the paper where I wrote the names. Luckily, I wasn't put in charge of notifying their families, but the officer who was quickly shared the names with me. "Caden Brown," I say, waiting for a response from her.

"I don't know him," Kelsey replies.

"Heather Smith"

"It doesn't ring a bell," she says.

"Bobby Goodwin."

Kelsey gasps. "Oh, no, not Bobby … I just talked with him last week."

"I'm sorry, baby," I say, feeling sad for her.

"Was he driving?" she asks. "He has dependency issues."

"No, he wasn't," I reply, thinking in the back of my mind that if he has dependency issues, the other kids probably do, too. I'm sure drugs or alcohol were involved. "The driver was a girl named Bridget Wilson."

"What?!" Kelsey shrieks. "No, not Bridget!"

Fuck! Now I remember that Bridget is the girl who reminds Kelsey of herself at that age. "Honey, I'm coming to get you. I'll take you to the hospital where they took her."

I find my supervisor and ask permission to leave. After I explain the situation, he allows me to go. I drive with lights and sirens all the way to Yelm to get Kelsey.

KELSEY

When Brady called to tell me about the accident, it was a roller coaster of emotions for me. First, to find out that students from my school had been involved was devastating. Then, I was relieved—although still concerned—to *not* know the first two kids he mentioned. When he said Bobby's name, my heart dropped. He's a troubled kid who's been couch surfing since his mom kicked him out a couple of months ago, and he self-medicates.

But when he said Bridget's name, tears sprung to my eyes, and I started to panic. Not my Bridget! She holds a special place in my heart, being so much like I was at that age. And now, just like me, she's been involved in a bad accident. I can't believe this happened to her, and I can only pray she's going to be okay.

I hear a knock on my door and grab my purse to leave, knowing it's Brady to pick me up. When I open the door and see him standing there in uniform, I'm momentarily struck by how handsome he looks.

"Hey," he says as I immediately walk out the door, closing and locking it behind me.

"Hey," I reply as I turn around to face him. He looks melancholy, sad, as if this accident has affected him in some way, too.

Or maybe he's just reacting to seeing me after our fight last night. I have to admit, it's been at the forefront of my mind all day, not knowing where our relationship stands now. I miss him. I thought a lot about our argument and his point of view of my situation. In his eyes, I'm hiding something from him, and he has no idea the amplitude of the situation. In my eyes, it's one of the worst things I could've done; I'm so ashamed, and I can't bring myself to share it with him.

Even with this tragedy looming before us, I can't stop wondering what he's thinking about us. I love him, and I want him in my life. I want to continue dating him and see where this goes. I can see myself living with him someday just as we talked about the other night, but I'm so afraid to tell him my secret.

Without saying another word, he wraps his arms around me in a hug. "Are you okay?" he asks as he holds me tight.

As I hold him back, I feel the tears coming. So many emotions are running through me right now, I don't even know what to say except, "Yeah."

He doesn't let go of me. We stand on my front step, enveloped in one another's arms, not saying anything, but at the same time, saying so much. I know he loves me, and he doesn't want to let me go any more than I want to let *him* go. He has become so special, so important to me over the past month, and I truly can't imagine my life without him now.

Then thoughts of Bridget cross my mind, and I know we need to go. I pull back from him and wipe my eyes. "We should get to the hospital," I say.

He nods, then leads me to his car. I don't know why, but I'm surprised to see his squad car, not his personal car, waiting for us. I haven't been in a police car since high school ... and I've never ridden in the front seat. He opens the passenger side door for me, and I slide in.

We don't talk much as he drives us to the hospital. Yelm doesn't have a hospital, so they transported the kids to Olympia. When we get there, Brady leads us because he knows where to go. When we get to a waiting room, I recognize Bridget's mom. We met once when she had to come pick Bridget up from school.

She's sitting alone, wearing sweats, a T-shirt, and a flannel. She looks disheveled, and I wonder if she has any support. I know she's a single mom who has had some financial problems, according to Bridget, but she works her ass off at one of the local diners. She looks distraught, as she should be, so I don't hesitate. I approach her and sit in the chair next to her. She looks up at me, and I can see tears in her eyes.

"Ms. Wilson, do you remember me? I'm Bridget's counselor at school. My name is Kelsey Richards."

She immediately starts crying and covers her face with her hands. Instinctually, I put my arm around her to comfort her, and we stay like that for some time. Five, maybe ten minutes pass, I don't know … all I know is that I'm glad I came, if only to help Bridget's mom through this.

When she finally stops sobbing and looks up at me with tears streaming down her face, she says, "I can't lose her. She's all I've got. I knew I shouldn't have let her go out tonight, but she wanted to be with her friends …" She pauses, then continues. "Am I a bad mom?"

"No," I say with conviction. "You are most definitely *not* a bad mom. Bridget has told me how you work hard to support her. If you were a bad mom, you wouldn't care. She loves you."

She starts to sob again, but this time, she leans into me, so I embrace her in a hug and let her cry some more. I can't believe this woman would be all alone if I wasn't here right now, and I feel for her. I can't imagine going through this trauma without any support.

I look up to find Brady sitting in a chair across from us. He's leaning forward, looking at the floor with his elbows propped on his knees. He looks sad, and I wish I could comfort him, too. But Bridget's mom needs it more than he does right now.

An hour passes, and we still haven't heard from the doctor. Another man and woman walk in, and I believe it's one of the other kids' parents. I don't know them, though I recognize the mom. She must've been at the school before. They don't interact or even acknowledge Bridget's mom, so I assume they've never met and don't know each other.

At last, a doctor walks into the waiting room and approaches us. "Ms. Wilson?"

She stands. "Yes. How is my daughter?"

"She's in recovery now. The surgery went well. She has a long road ahead of her, but I believe she'll be okay." He then goes on to explain the extent of her injuries. I'm so relieved to hear she's going to be okay! I look over at Brady, and he gives me a small smile. I smile in return, then turn back to the doctor.

"You'll be able to see her once they get her settled in her recovery room in ICU," he says to Bridget's mom. "A nurse will come get you then and take you to her. Do you have any questions?"

She shakes her head. "No, I don't think so. I'm just so relieved!"

The doctor turns and leaves the room, and Bridget's mom turns to me. "Thank God she's going to be all right!" She covers her face with her hands, and I can tell she's crying again. I stand and wrap her in another hug.

The man and woman who came into the waiting room walk over to us. "Excuse me," the woman says. Her eyes are bloodshot as if she's been crying. "I didn't mean to eavesdrop, but I over-heard what the doctor was telling you. Was your daughter in the car accident in Tenino?"

"Yes," Ms. Wilson replies with a nod.

The other woman tears up again. "Our son was in the car with your daughter. His name is Caden."

I leave the two of them to talk and slip away to sit by Brady. "Are you okay?" he asks when I sit next to him.

I nod. "I'm so relieved Bridget is going to be okay. I just hope the others are, too."

Brady takes my hand. I look at him, and for the first time since we got here, I notice he looks uneasy.

"Are you okay?" I ask him.

"Yeah, I'm fine," he replies, but the way he darted his eyes away, then back to me again, tells me he's not being completely honest.

Before I can ask any further questions, Ms. Wilson and the other parents approach us. "Excuse us, officer," the dad says to Brady. "We just noticed you're a Tenino officer. Were you at the accident?"

Brady stands to talk to them. "I was, but unfortunately, I didn't do anything except stop traffic. I don't have any answers for you. I'm sorry."

"Oh, well, thanks anyway," the dad says, looking confused. "Can I ask why you're here, then?"

Brady explains, "Well, when I found out the kids in the car were students at Yelm High, I contacted my girlfriend here." He turns and points at me, and I get up from the chair and stand next to him. "She is one of the school's counselors. She was extremely concerned about the students involved, so I brought her here."

The other mom unexpectedly steps toward me, hugging me tight. "Thank you for being here," she says. "Thank you for caring so much." When she steps away from me, she wipes her eyes again.

"Do you know Caden Brown?" the dad asks me.

"No, I haven't had the chance to meet Caden yet. I'm new to the school this year."

I chat with Caden's parents and Bridget's mom for a few minutes. Brady stepped away and sat back in the chair he was in, and when I get the chance to look back at him, I see that he still looks uneasy. His elbows are on his knees, he's looking down at the ground, and he's bouncing one of his feet in a nervous motion. I can't help but wonder what's bothering him. He can't be this uneasy just because of our fight. Something else must be on his mind.

Another doctor walks into the room and gives Caden's parents good news as well, and then a nurse comes to take Bridget's mom to her room. I say my goodbyes to all three of them, then turn back to Brady. "Do you want to go?" I ask.

He looks up at me. "Yeah, if you're ready."

We walk out of the hospital, and he takes my hand in his. "I got a text from another officer," he says as we walk toward his car. "He said that the other two kids were in the back seat of the car, and their injuries weren't as severe, so they were taken to the hospital in Centralia."

I nod. "That makes sense. I was wondering why their parents weren't here." Centralia is actually closer to the scene of the accident, but it's a smaller hospital. Trauma cases are always transported to the larger hospital in Olympia, which is just a little farther away.

He opens the passenger side door for me, but I don't get in the car. I stop and look at him. "What's wrong, Brady?"

"What do you mean?"

"You were visibly upset in that waiting room. I didn't think you were so emotionally invested in the kids involved."

Brady shrugs. "I don't know. I care because they're kids, and they're students at your school. You care, so I care."

I want to believe him, but I don't. My gut tells me something else is going on with him. "Tell me the truth."

Brady takes his arm off the car door and stands straight. "I *am* telling you the truth. Nothing is wrong."

I eye him, and he breaks eye contact first. "Let's go," he says. Then he turns and walks to the other side of the car. He gets in, so I get in the car, too.

But I don't drop the conversation. I need to know what's bothering him.

"Are you okay?" I ask, and suddenly, I wonder if he's second-guessing our relationship. "Are *we* okay?"

"I'm fine," he says, and his stern tone lets me know he doesn't want to talk about this. "And I don't know ... you tell me if we're okay."

I cock an eyebrow. "I hope we're okay," I reply. "I still love you, and unless you've changed your mind since our texts earlier, you still love me."

Brady glances at me for a second before turning his attention back to the road. "I *do* love you," he says, his tone calmer now. "I'm sorry about last night. You can take all the time you need to tell me your secret. And if you never feel ready ... well, then I'll have to accept that."

Though I'm surprised by his words, I'm also relieved. However, the mystery of what's really bothering him, as well as the real reason he left Portland, is still bothering me. I mull it over in my mind as Brady drives us back to Yelm. The bottom line is, if I really want to know his secrets, I'm going to have to tell him mine. I just don't know if I'm ready to do that.

We ride in silence all the way back home. When he parks the car in front of my apartment, I turn to him. I have to do this, and if I don't do it now, I don't think I ever will.

"Brady," I say, and he turns to me. "You know I was addicted to drugs in high school ..."

"Yeah ..." he says, looking confused as to why I'm telling him this again.

"Well ... drugs cost money ... and I didn't have a job..." I look down. I can't look at him when I say this.

"Okay ... so what are you saying?" he asks.

"I paid for my habit in other ways," I explain, leaving my words hang in the air for him to interpret on his own.

Brady doesn't say anything. When I can't stand the silence any longer, I look at him. "Are you going to say anything?"

He knits his eyebrows together. "What are you saying exactly, Kelsey? How did you pay for your drugs?"

I guess he couldn't read between the lines like I hoped he would. Either that, or he just wants to hear me say the words I don't want to say out loud. I take a deep breath, then close my eyes and quietly say, "Sex."

Again silence. I open my eyes and see Brady looking away from me, staring out the front windshield. I can't tell what he's thinking, and it scares me to death. He taps his thumb on top of the steering wheel.

"Say something," I whisper. "What are you thinking?"

Brady looks back at me and clears his throat. "You had sex for drugs?" he asks, his voice eerily calm.

I nod and look down. Holy shit! Did I just tell him the worst part of my life? I can't believe I said the words out loud, yet I also feel a weight lifted. He knows now. If he decides he can't be with me because of this, then I guess it's better to know now rather than months down the road.

I decide to elaborate a little more. "You see, it started with my boyfriend at the time. Like I told you before, I don't remember losing my virginity. After that, I figured sex was just sex; if I couldn't even remember my first time, then why should it matter? The bottom line was, I wanted to get high more than I cared about anything else."

Brady doesn't say anything, but then I feel his hand under my chin, slowly bringing my head up until our eyes meet. Without warning, Brady kisses me, taking me completely by surprise. His mouth covers mine, kissing me slow and sweet. Relief washes over me; this is a better response than I expected.

Our kiss goes on and on, his tongue caressing mine and his

hands stroking my hair gently. I grip his upper arms, clinging to him. I don't want to lose Brady. He means so much to me now.

When he does pull his lips away, he rests his forehead against mine. "Baby, I'm so sorry you went through all that when you were younger. As I told you before, the past doesn't matter now. That was years ago, and you're not that lost teenage girl anymore. I love you; the woman you've become is so inspirational."

"Thank you," I say, my voice cracking as my eyes tear up. I close my eyes and bite my tongue, trying to stop myself from crying.

I feel Brady pull back from me, so I open my eyes. He's sitting back in his seat, staring out the window again his left elbow resting on the door. He's biting the tip of his thumb as if he's nervous.

"What is it?" I ask, now worried about what he could possibly be thinking.

Brady turns to me again but keeps his eyes down. He takes a deep breath, then says, "I had to leave Portland."

"Why?" I automatically ask. Is he going to tell me the truth now that I've told him my secret?

"Some of my closest buddies were involved in a shooting about a year and a half ago. Three of them were shot and survived. Another one wasn't so lucky." He closes his eyes and pinches the bridge of his nose. I place my hand on his knee to comfort him. "After that happened, I kept thinking it could be me next. I mean, all they were doing was responding to a call, and they were ambushed. That could've happened to any of us."

"I'm so sorry," I say, offering my condolences.

"And then it happened again," he says solemnly, his eyes looking up at me.

Suddenly, I remember this now. It was all over the news! Jesus Christ, why didn't I think of this before? It was so sad. Portland suffered two officer shootings in one year. It was a devastating loss.

"Oh, my God," I whisper. "I remember hearing about this."

Brady nods and looks down again. "The second shooting was gang related. Four officers were hit that time, and two died. Losing three brothers in one year was more than just a tragedy. I can't even explain the loss all of us in the department felt, and that fear was still with me. I had trouble going to work, and I knew I needed a change."

I squeeze his knee, and he takes my hand in his. We sit in silence for a few minutes. I feel a mixture of emotions; relief that we told our secrets, shame for what I did as a teen, and sadness for what he went through. Not only all that, but I'm still reeling from everything that happened tonight with Bridget and the other kids from school.

Finally, Brady looks up at me again. "My dad got me the job with Tenino. He knew I needed to get out of the city, and I'm so glad he helped me. I love my job; I just couldn't do it there anymore."

"That makes sense, and what a great thing for your dad to do."

Brady rubs his thumb across the top of my hand. "Yeah, but it also made me feel weak. Like I couldn't handle being a cop in Portland, so I had to come home and take a job my dad got me. Although I'm happy about the change now, it still kind of bothers me, so I don't like to talk about it. As far as everyone is concerned, I just wanted to move home and be closer to my family."

Just as he did to me a moment ago, I cup his chin in my free hand to get his attention. "Brady, you are an amazing man. Your job is extremely taxing and stressful. You are not weak. Not at all. You did the right thing to keep yourself sane."

"Thank you," he says, his voice soft.

"Your secret is safe with me, baby," I tell him, and then I lean in to kiss him.

We eventually make it out of his car and into my apartment.

It's late, and we're both exhausted, so we go to bed and go to sleep.

BRADY

*W*aking up next to Kelsey is the best feeling. I love it when she's the last thing I see before I go to bed and the first thing I see in the morning. I love her. Finding out her secret last night didn't change how I felt about her. In fact, it made me love her more. I feel for her, having gone through all that at such a young age, but she has turned into an amazing woman. I felt so relieved she finally told me her secret that I had to tell her mine.

Last night was the first night we slept together without having sex first. We were both so exhausted from the events of the day, and we just needed to sleep. In some weird way, it made me feel even closer to her. Just cuddling and comforting one another can often feel more intimate than having sex.

Kelsey's eyes open, and I admire how adorable she is when she's just waking up. She rubs her eyes and combs her fingers through her hair, her eyes only half open. I can't help myself and reach for her, putting my arm around her and kissing her senseless. She moans into my mouth, kissing me back, and her hands embrace me as well.

My mouth travels to her neck, kissing her gently as I slowly move down her body. I lift the T-shirt she's wearing, and she pulls it off. I kiss her breasts, and she sucks in a breath. Before I know it, her hand is snaking its way into my boxer briefs and pulling them down. She wraps a hand around my dick and starts stroking me up and down. "Kelsey," I rasp out.

Kissing my way back up her body to her neck, I lightly bite her. She squirms, and I can tell it drives her crazy. Her hands start roaming my body, and my hands start roaming hers. I dip a hand inside her panties and slide two fingers inside her. She moans, and I roll us over so she's on top. She rides my fingers, hovering over me.

"You're quite the wake-up call," she says, kissing my neck.

She continues to move up and down on my fingers. I rub her clit with my thumb, but I can tell it's not enough. She whispers in my ear, "I need more."

I shift, moving my hand so I can pull down her silky underwear. Then I slide mine off as well. She positions herself over my lap and sinks down. My hands guide her body, touching her gently, feeling her soft skin. She rides me hard and fast, which is just what I need right now. She's right; this is quite a wake-up call.

"Brady." She moans my name, then leans down to kiss me.

As good as it feels to have her on top, I need to feel in control right now. Again, I flip us over so I'm on top. I pound into her, and she angles her hips so I slide in deeper. Her body feels so good, and I get lost in the feeling.

As I kiss her shoulder, her head moves back against the pillow. She's in ecstasy, and I hope I can always be the man to make her feel this way. I love her more than any woman I've ever known.

"I love you," I rasp out, kissing her neck once more.

"I love you," she says, her breathy voice letting me know she's close to letting go.

Her nails dig into my skin. I move at a faster pace, wanting to make her come.

When I feel her inner muscles clench, she lets out a sexy cry, coming hard. It doesn't take me long to follow.

We lie together, holding each other for a few moments.

"I really do love you, Kelsey," I tell her, suddenly feeling the need to explain how much she means to me.

"I love you, too, Brady," she replies, running a hand through my hair.

"No, I need you to know something," I say, leaning up so I can look her in the eye when I say this. "After you told me your secret last night, I fell even deeper in love with you than I was before. You continue to amaze me with your story. You're a fascinating woman who has defeated the odds and made something of yourself after going through some terrible times. I knew I could trust you with my own secret, and I just hope you still feel the same way about me."

"Thank you," she whispers, then clears her throat, blinking back tears. "Brady, I love you so much. I never thought I would get the opportunity to love and be loved in this way. You make me feel something I've never felt before, and I feel incredibly lucky that you're as understanding as you are. My past isn't ideal, and the fact that you look past that means so much to me. I love you."

I dip my head down to kiss her again. I don't think I'll ever get enough of this woman, and I can't wait to see what the future brings for us.

EPILOGUE

Kelsey

*I*t's the Fourth of July again—one year since I first saw Brady at Nolan's house—and so much has happened over this past year. I can't believe how much my life has changed.

Brady and I moved in together last month. Our leases were up, so we found a small house that's perfect for us. It's nice being out of the apartment complex and having more space, and living with Brady has been better than I could have imagined.

Our relationship has grown so much since that night we confessed our secrets. We don't have anything to hide from each other, and I know I can trust him and tell him anything.

Speaking of that night in November, Bridget, Caden, the other kids involved in the accident, as well as the people in the other car, all made full recoveries. Bridget had two broken legs, a broken arm, and several cuts and bruises that had to heal. Unfortunately, she was charged with a DUI, but it forced her to get the help she needed, and she is now sober. She's doing homeschool through an online program, and she's doing very well. Even though she's no longer a student at Yelm, she still keeps in contact with me to let me know how she's doing. Her mom was so grateful that I stayed with her in the hospital waiting room, and we've also become friends.

I feel a sense of joy I've never felt before. I never realized just how much my past was holding me back. Now, I'm more confident in all aspects of my life. It's as if telling my secret cleansed my soul. After telling Brady everything, I knew there was nothing stopping me anymore.

As Brady drives us to Nolan's house, I reflect on how happy I am with this man. We've talked about getting married someday, but we're not in a hurry. We're committed to each other, and it's even more wonderful that my family loves him, and his family loves me. At Christmas, I got the chance to meet his brother Gary and his wife and kids. I got along well with his wife, Gina, and they treated me like family. In April, Brady's other brother, Mike, came to visit with his family. They were very nice, and I also hit it off with his wife, Whitney. Brady and I are planning to visit each of his brothers sometime in the next year.

It's still funny to me that Brady's dad arrested me, but there's never any awkward feelings around him. He's a forgiving man, and he knows I'm not that addicted teenager anymore.

When we arrive at the party, Emmy greets us at the door. "Kelsey!" she exclaims, jumping at me. We hug, and just like every time I see her, I can't believe how big she's getting.

She lets go of me and turns to Brady. She has warmed up to him over the past several months. Knowing that he's friends with her dad helped her feel comfortable around him pretty quickly. "Hi!" she says to him, then also wraps him in a hug.

"Hey, Emmy. How are you today?" he asks, hugging her in return.

"I'm good! I can't wait for the fireworks later!" she says with the kind of excitement only a four-year-old can muster.

"Me, too," he says, then winks at her. She smiles and then runs off toward the back of the house. We follow her, finding the party.

"You're here!" Teresa exclaims. She's standing behind the kitchen island covered in platters of food.

"Hi!" Brady and I both say at the same time.

Teresa rounds the island and gives us each a hug. "It's so good to see you guys. Help yourselves to some food. Drinks are in the coolers outside, along with the burgers and hot dogs Nolan is barbecuing."

"Thanks," I reply. "Are Mom and Dad here?"

"Yeah, they're outside, too," she replies, and then Nolan is calling her name from the back deck. "He must need a plate for the burgers. Make yourselves at home!" Teresa grabs an empty plate off the counter and heads outside. Brady and I skip the food for now and go outside. We find Mom and Dad and sit with them.

The afternoon is enjoyable, talking with family and friends, as well as eating delicious food. Nolan put up a badminton net, so Brady and I play a game against Nolan and Teresa. Then Emmy and I play against Brady. We win.

When it's finally dark enough, Nolan, Dad, and Brady get the fireworks show ready. Everyone else positions chairs on the lawn for a good view. Emmy, as well as a few other kids here with their parents, can't sit still; they're jumping up and down, barely able to contain their excitement for the fireworks.

As the show starts, everyone oohs and aahs at the beautiful colors lighting up the night sky. Not only do we see Nolan's show, but several other neighbors are setting their own off as well. The sky is full of beautiful twinkling lights, which is why I don't even notice Brady approach me.

Sensing someone next to me, I turn to look who it is, and I'm startled to see him.

Isn't he helping Dad and Nolan right now? Why is he over here?

"Hi," he says, then kisses my cheek. He's kneeling on the ground, so he's at the same level I am in the chair I'm sitting in.

"Hi," I say, confused. "What are you doing here?"

Brady smiles. "They didn't really need my help, so I thought I'd admire the show with you."

"Oh," I say, and then everyone around us gasps. We both look up to see a beautiful pink firework.

We continue watching the show, and then Brady shifts, turning so he's in front of me now, not next to me. "Kelsey," he says, taking my hand in his. "A year ago today, we met, and I was overwhelmed by your beauty, witty personality, and smarts."

I stare at him, unsure why he's saying this to me right now while also realizing how incredibly romantic he's being.

"I knew something special would happen between us. I just regret it took us three months to get there. However, that doesn't matter now because with you, I'm happier than I've ever been before."

Brady reaches into his shorts pocket, and it's at that moment that I realize he's down on one knee. Holy shit! Is he really doing this right now?

When he pulls his hand out of his pocket, he presents me with the most beautiful ring I've ever seen. My hands fly to my face, tears springing to my eyes.

"Kelsey, will you make me the luckiest man alive and be my wife?"

More fireworks go off, but my attention is solely on Brady. I love this man, and I can't imagine my life without him. Of course, I'll marry him!

I reach for him, sitting on the edge of my chair, and place my hands on each side of his face. "Yes, baby. I would love to be your wife!" I lean in and kiss him on the lips.

Suddenly, everyone at the party erupts in cheers. Brady and I pull apart, looking around us.

"Put the ring on her!" Nolan yells, and everyone laughs, including us.

Brady takes my left hand and slips the engagement ring onto my finger. I look at it in amazement, never thinking this would be a possibility for me. I reach for Brady and kiss him again, and everyone around us cheers as fireworks light up the sky. My life is better than I ever imagined it could be, and I'm happier than I ever thought was possible. I love Brady more and more every day, and I can't wait to see what the future holds for us.

The End

ALSO BY C.L. COLLIER

Discovering Us Series

Stacking the Deck

Finding Our Rhythm

Meant to Be

What I Never Knew Series

What I Never Knew

What I Never Knew I Wanted

What I Never Knew I Needed

The Vagabond Series

Passion in Paris - this book also has connections to Stacking the Deck!

Belize Bliss

The Salvation Society

Harbor

Summers in Seaside Series

Summer Magic

Summer Love (A Summers in Seaside and Seasons of Love Crossover)

Seasons of Love Series

Holly

Summer Love (A Summers in Seaside and Seasons of Love Crossover)

Autumn (coming soon in the Love and Coffee multi-author anthology)

April (coming in 2024!)

Hot Vegas Nights Series

<u>Playing Vegas</u>

Visit C.L. Collier's web site

COMING SOON FROM C.L. COLLIER

Hopelessly Devoted: A Romance Anthology to Benefit Women's Cancer Research - coming September 7, 2023

Love and Coffee: A Limited Edition Contemporary Romance Anthology - coming September 19, 2023

Let's Get Naughty 2: A Limited Edition Romance Anthology - coming October 24, 2023

Stud Finder: A Limited Edition Romance Anthology - coming February 6, 2024

C.L. Collier's newsletter - Stay tuned for more!

ACKNOWLEDGMENTS

Thank you, Amanda Shelley, for being my writing buddy! We haven't been able to connect as often as we used to, but I want you to know how much I value your opinion, your help, and your friendship!

Thank you to my editor, Jenny Sims, for putting up with me and this book! I don't know if I ever truly met a deadline this time around, but you certainly did an amazing job with my edits, regardless. I appreciate the hard work you always put into your editing!

Finally, thank you to my readers! I dedicate this book to you because I truly appreciate you reading my words!

ABOUT THE AUTHOR

C.L. Collier is a USA Today Bestselling Author who lives in the beautiful Pacific Northwest. She was raised in the Seattle area, and although she lives closer to Portland, Oregon now, she frequently visits the hometown she loves. When she's not writing, you can find her reading, watching her favorite sports teams, spending time with her family, or going to concerts. She likes her music loud, wine and coffee sweet, and her books steamy.